THE MIGHTY

The Voyage on the Oddest Sea

CRISPIN BOYER

Illustrated by Andy Elkerton

UNDER THE Stars

NATIONAL
GEOGRAPHIC

Washington, D.C.

NATIONAL GEOGRAPHIC and Yellow Border Design are trademarks of the National Geographic Society, used under license.

Under the Stars is a trademark of National Geographic Partners, LLC.

Since 1888, the National Geographic Society has funded more than 14,000 research, conservation, education, and storytelling projects around the world. National Geographic Partners distributes a portion of the funds it receives from your purchase to National Geographic Society to support programs including the conservation of animals and their habitats. To learn more, visit natgeo.com/info.

For more information, visit nationalgeographic.com, call 1-877-873-6846, or write to the following address:

National Geographic Partners, LLC
1145 17th Street NW
Washington, DC 20036-4688 U.S.A.

For librarians and teachers: nationalgeographic.com/books/librarians-and-educators

More for kids from National Geographic: natgeokids.com

For rights or permissions inquiries, please contact National Geographic Books Subsidiary Rights: bookrights@natgeo.com

Designed by Amanda Larsen
Hand-lettering by Jay Roeder

Library of Congress Cataloging-in-Publication Data
Names: Boyer, Crispin, author.
Title: The voyage on the Oddest Sea / Crispin Boyer.
Description: Washington, D.C. : National Geographic Kids, [2023] | Series: Zeus the mighty ; 5 | Audience: Ages 8-12. | Audience: Grades 4-6.
Identifiers: LCCN 2022003540 (print) | LCCN 2022003541 (ebook) | ISBN 9781426373510 (hardcover) | ISBN 9781426374340 (library binding) | ISBN 9781426375811 (ebook)
Subjects: CYAC: Pets--Fiction. | Octopuses--Fiction. | Mythology, Greek--Fiction. | Adventure and adventurers--Fiction. | Pet shops--Fiction. | LCGFT: Animal fiction.
Classification: LCC PZ7.1.B6947 Vo 2023 (print) | LCC PZ7.1.B6947 (ebook) | DDC [Fic]--dc23
LC record available at https://lccn.loc.gov/2022003540
LC ebook record available at https://lccn.loc.gov/2022003541

Printed in the United States of America
23/WOR/1

For Paul Sr. the Heroic

—C.B.

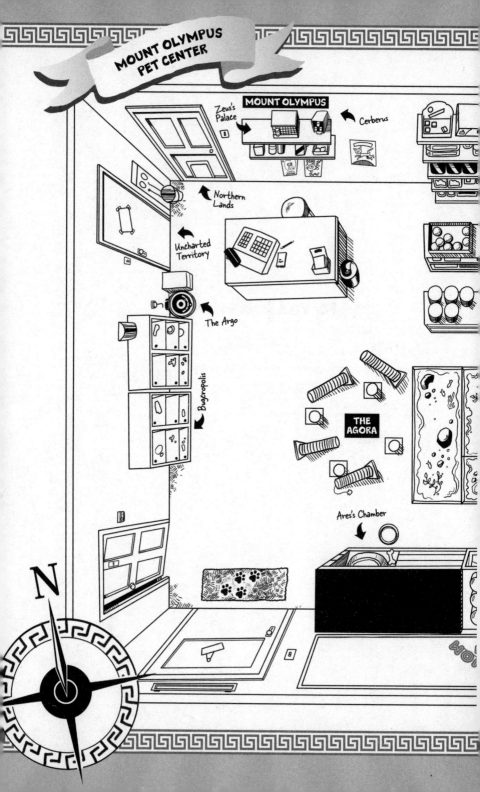

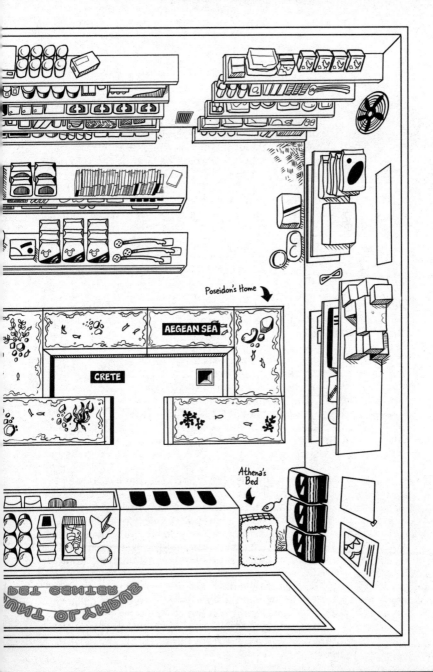

CAST OF CHARACTERS

Zeus is a golden hamster with a cloud-shaped patch on his cheek. Zeus believes he's the king of all the other animals that live at the Mount Olympus Pet Center. The favorite rescued pet of Artie, the shop's owner, Zeus genuinely cares about his fellow Olympians but also sees them as minions that should follow him on nightly adventures, which often go awry. When humans aren't around, he scrambles down from "Mount Olympus," the highest shelf in the shop where his enclosure is, and pictures himself wearing a white chiton—a fine shirt people wore in ancient Greece—and a crown-like gilded laurel wreath.

Demeter is a small grasshopper with a big heart. Once a resident of the pet center's Bugcropolis (the city of insects), she's now Zeus's constant, loyal companion and loves to explore the shop's world. She wears a sash of lettuce over her shoulder and a laurel wreath on her head to represent the Greek goddess of the harvest, for whom she's named. The youngest and fastest of the Olympians, Demeter can fly in short bursts. But don't let her size fool you—this is one courageous grasshopper!

Athena is the wise gray tabby cat that lives under the front window of Mount Olympus Pet Center. Named after the goddess of wisdom, Athena often tries to keep Zeus out of trouble when he starts dreaming up wild adventures. Her quick and clever thinking helps settle arguments and solve problems. For instance, she figured out how to steer the *Argo*, a robot vacuum, which now captains around the pet center. In the human world, she wears a gold collar with an owl charm, but the other Olympians see her wearing a laurel crown and two thin gold bracelets that wrap around her front paws.

Ares the pug is the strongest of the pet center Olympians. Courageous and impulsive like the god of war, Ares is the first to jump into an adventure and face any monster. But his excitement can sometimes get the better of him. (One time he accidentally sat on Poseidon's hose and almost suffocated the pufferfish!) Ares loves to be called a good boy and can eat an entire handful of Mutt Nuggets in one sitting, which probably contributes to his "meatloaf-ish" body. He wears a spiked collar and, among the Olympians, a bronze Spartan war helmet.

Poseidon is a white-spotted pufferfish that lives in the fish tank (known to the animals as the Aegean Sea) at Mount Olympus Pet Center. From his saltwater throne, Poseidon rules over his fishy minions and challenges Zeus's authority over the center. The two regularly argue over who is the better ruler. Poseidon can leave his aquarium by swimming into a plastic diving helmet that has a long hose connected to the tank. He wears a tiny gold crown and carries a trident, just like the Greek god he's named after.

Hermes is the newest resident of Mount Olympus Pet Center. Rescued from a poultry ranch, she's an Appenzeller hen (or lady chicken). Ancient Greece is a new realm for Hermes, but that doesn't stop her from trying to live up to her name as the goddess of sleep. She can crow out a tune that would wake the dead! Hermes has the courage of an Amazon and helps the team soar to new heights—even if she's afraid of heights herself.

Artemis "Artie" Ambrosia is the owner of Mount Olympus Pet Center. In Greek mythology Artemis is the goddess of hunting and wild animals—so it makes sense that Artie has rescued the animals living at the center. It also makes sense that she named all her rescued animals after Greek gods, since she loves Greek mythology. She even listens to *Greeking Out*, a podcast that retells the famous myths and gives the animals crazy ideas for their adventures. Artie plans to open a rescue center next door to Mount Olympus so she can find *fur*-ever homes for more animals.

PREFACE

ARTEMIS AMBROSIA WAS USED TO FEELING
tiny brown eyes boring into the top of her head as she
sat behind the cash register of Mount Olympus Pet
Center. "Whatever you're planning up there, Zeus,"
she said without looking up, "don't bother."

The hamster on the shelf above squeaked and
scurried away from the bars of his habitat. He curled
up on a fleece bed that matched his golden fur.

"Chatting with your troublemaking rodent again,
Artie?" asked a sandy-haired woman standing in the
doorway to the shop space next door.

"I wish I could speak hamster, Callie," Artie replied.
"Might help me solve some mysteries around here."

Callie set down her tool bag and surveyed Artie's
favorite rescues—the gray cat pawing at a ball of
string in front of the counter, a speckled hen pecking
at the end of the string, a tan pug gnawing on a rubber
bone nearby. "I dunno." She shrugged. "Life got pretty

normal once we learned how your hamster was escaping every night."

Artie reached up and tugged at the piece of twine locking the back door of Zeus's habitat, then switched on the security camera Callie had installed and later repaired after Zeus broke it. Red, white, and purple lights flashed across the camera port as it began panning in an arc that scanned Zeus's home. The hamster glared back. The patch of white fur on his cheek quivered.

"You won't be trapped in there forever, Zeus." Artie patted a pile of clear plastic tubes, which would soon become a new floor display. A nearby box showed the same tubes connected into an elaborate network of tunnels with scurrying rodents.

"Want me to set up that hamster-tunnel thing for the little guy?" Callie asked.

"Nah. We have a bigger project on the list for tonight!" Artie checked the time on her phone and headed for the front door.

Callie chuckled as she followed Artie out. "We might actually get some stuff done now that Zeus isn't breaking out every night."

CHAPTER 1

ZEUS THE MIGHTY WAS BREAKING OUT tonight.

"They're gone!" The hamster hopped from his Golden Fleece bed and hurried around his palace atop Mount Olympus, the tallest spot in Greece.

"Are we sure they're gone?" asked the grasshopper raiding Zeus's food bowl for a fresh piece of lettuce.

"I'm sure they're not here now, Demeter!" Zeus snapped. "Olympians, assemble! Escape Plan Achilles!"

Below, Ares the pug spit out his rubber bone and tilted his head quizzically, his Spartan war helmet nearly flopping off. "Achilles ...? Didn't we try that one already? The one where Zeus's palace almost slid off Mount Olympus?"

"No, that was Escape Plan Icarus," corrected Hermes the hen. She was still fiddling with the end of Athena's string, scratching the waddles beneath her chin with it. "Or was that Neptune? Which plan ended up with Zeus nearly drowning?"

"Doesn't matter!" Zeus interrupted, his voice booming from far above. "Those plans were all practice for this one! Escape Plan Achilles is perfect—perfect!" He reached behind his water bottle and pulled out a crude life-size replica of himself. It was made from sticks and stuffing crammed into the mangy lion hide known as the Nemean cloak and was dressed in one of Zeus's spare robe-like chitons.

"It's your time to shine, Zeus Deuce!" Zeus said to his clone. He licked his paw and smoothed out the white piece of pillow fluff on Zeus Deuce's cheek, then turned his attention to Greece. "Olympians, prepare the snare."

At the base of the mountain, Athena the cat batted her ball of string to Hermes, who handed the loose end to Ares to grab with his mouth. Hermes then took the ball in both wings and heaved it high above her, watching it unravel as it traveled. Zeus reached his paws through the pillars of his palace and snatched the now much smaller string ball from midair, holding it just outside the palace. He turned to the grasshopper, who was wrapping her lettuce leaf over one shoulder like a sash. "Demeter, play with your food later! Take this string and put a leash on that guard mutt!"

Demeter squeezed through the pillars next to Zeus and grabbed the small string ball. She ran along the narrow cliff in front of the palace toward a four-sided structure with smooth gray walls: the doghouse of Cerberus. Demeter had never caught the attention of the three-headed guard dog of Hades, and she didn't now. The doorway to Cerberus's house remained dark, the beast brooding inside. She looped the string around the house, watching it cinch tight as the house panned back and forth. Then Demeter darted around the rear of the palace. She slipped through the bars of the secured back door and handed the string back to Zeus.

Zeus tied the string to Zeus Deuce with a knot. He propped his doppelgänger against his exercise wheel. *POP!* One of Zeus Deuce's eyes—a piece of Fuzzy Feast—fell off.

"That part of Escape Plan Achilles?" Demeter smirked.

Ignoring her, Zeus hastily stuck the eye back on and straightened the piece of golden string that served as his replica's laurel crown. Addressing the Olympians he said, "Tonight's the night, gang. The last couple of escape plans didn't pan out for two reasons: We couldn't get the back door open. And we couldn't get past Hades's annoying watchdog."

"And all the accidents," Ares chimed in. "Don't forget the accidents."

"And just a basic breakdown in communication," Athena added.

Zeus shushed them. "Point is, this plan takes care of everything." He focused on Ares. "War god, when I count down from three, make a run for it!"

"Gotcha, boss!" Ares said enthusiastically around the string in his mouth. The pug leaned low on his front legs, his spiked collar clunking against the ground, and prepared to sprint.

"Three!" Zeus said.

Athena perked up her furry gray ears. "Wait, does this plan really take care of everything?"

"Two!" Ares dug his rear paws into the ground.

"I mean, when Ares takes off," Athena continued, "won't he just yank Zeus Deuce into the back door?"

Zeus sighed loudly and paused his countdown. "Yeah ... and?"

"Won't that, you know, break your clone into a

million bits?" Athena asked skeptically.

"It's the door that'll break into a million bits."
Zeus held up his doppelgänger for Athena's inspection.
"You do know this cloak is indestructible, right?"

Athena studied the ratty lion's fur and narrowed her
blue eyes. "Is it though?"

"ONE!" Zeus exclaimed, finishing his countdown.

Ares took off, but as suddenly as he bolted, the
ground beneath him began shifting. Nearby crates
tumbled. Across Greece, mountainsides rumbled.
Ares stumbled, spitting out the string.

Athena sank low. "Earthquake!" she yelled.

CHAPTER 2

ZEUS GRABBED ONTO THE PILLARS OF his palace. Demeter shot out four legs to keep her balance.

A clanking sound behind them caught Zeus's attention. The back door of his palace had shaken off its hinges. Now it dangled from the twine that Artie had wrapped around it.

"Hey!" Zeus stepped toward the exit but stumbled as the floor beneath him rattled and shook. He noticed with alarm that the entire palace was jittering toward the edge of the mountaintop. But the palace wasn't the only object moving with the seismic waves. Zeus watched as Cerberus's guardhouse skittered closer and closer to the edge—until it plummeted over the side.

Just as suddenly as it started, the rumbling faded. The palace settled, one corner hanging over the edge of the mountaintop. "Hah!" Zeus cackled triumphantly as he let go of the pillar. And then he noticed the string, one end of which was still attached to Zeus Deuce, and the other end of which was still attached to Cerberus. It was spooling fast off the mountaintop, its slack paying out through the back of his palace. "Huh."

TWING! The string stretched taut. Zeus's doppelgänger zipped across the floor and disappeared out the now open back door.

Demeter watched Zeus Deus vanish over the edge of Mount Olympus, but then something far more

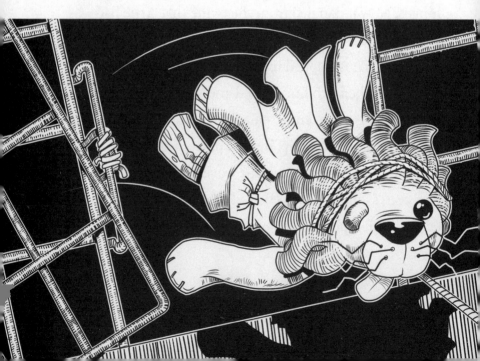

interesting caught her eye. "Um, Zeus," she said in a low voice. "You seeing what I'm seeing?"

"I know, right?" He darted through the door and stood just outside his palace. "I'm free!" He ran to the edge of Mount Olympus and peered at Cerberus's guard hut, broken and dark at the foot of the mountain far below. "Told you Escape Plan Achilles would work!" He clapped his paws and began skipping around the mountaintop.

"Not sure now is the time to celebrate," Demeter said, as she gazed out over Greece.

"Oh, quit being such a party poop—" Zeus skidded to a halt. Their usual vista had been transformed. Crates and artifacts had tumbled down the mountainsides of rocky Greece in a dozen avalanches. The rope-wrapped pillars of their meeting place, the Agora, had tipped over in all directions. A pile of clear tubes had collapsed, sending plastic tunnels rolling across Greece. But the biggest change by far wasn't on land. The Aegean Sea, roiling with sloshing waves, had doubled in size.

"What in blazes?!" Zeus was dumbfounded.

CHAPTER 3

AFTER THE QUAKING SUBSIDED, THE surface of the Aegean returned to its usual calm. The sea now stretched much farther west than before, flooding the area that had been home to the Agora and stretching closer to the Bugcropolis, the city of insects and Demeter's hometown.

As Zeus scanned this strange new landscape, he was surprised to see Artie and Callie standing at the Aegean's southern shore.

"Guess they didn't leave after all," Demeter said softly from inside the palace.

Zeus suddenly remembered where he was, gawking at the cliff edge of Mount Olympus. "Eeek!" He darted through his back door, which he carefully shifted so it appeared to be secure. The last thing he needed was to get caught out and about just moments after recovering his freedom.

Fortunately for Zeus, the two women were too busy to notice. "We need to slide it to the left just a tad," Artie said, eyeballing the new aquarium they had just dragged into the pet center, "so I can line it up with the other tanks."

"Easy for you to say," Callie replied, rolling out her shoulders and gripping one side of the large rectangular tank while Artie grabbed the other side. "Ready when you are."

"Heave!" Artie exclaimed.

The two women leaned into the tank and shoved it a few inches along the floor. Once again, the pet center rumbled and displays shook. A rack of cat-grooming accessories toppled. Water sloshed over the sides of the tank. Zeus's habitat began jittering toward the edge of the shelf again, moments from teetering into the brink. "There! Right there!" Artie said breathlessly. She tightened the plumbing that connected the new tank to the rest of the pet center's saltwater aquarium system. Meanwhile, the rumbling subsided. Zeus's habitat settled, a full quarter of it hanging off its shelf.

Panting, Callie looked around at the pet center and all the tumbled displays. "Well, that made a mess."

Artie was fiddling with a loose air hose on the tank's filter. The long, tentacle-like hose whipped through the water like an electrified spaghetti noodle, almost as if it was alive. She was trying to secure the slimy hose to the filter, but it kept slipping from her grip. "A hundred gallons of salt water is no small thing to lug around," she said. "Same thing happened the last time I added to the fish section."

Callie leaned over and peered into the tank. On its sandy bottom she spotted a few corals, some swaying green seagrass, and a little treasure chest that opened and closed with explosions of bubbles. Rock sculptures formed mountains and canyons, crisscrossing the aquarium floor. "Nice digs. Who's moving in?"

"Ooh, glad you asked!" Artie abandoned her battle with the filter hose, leaving it to twist in the water, and walked to the door to the expansion. "Give me a minute to grab our new eight-armed friend."

CHAPTER 4

"EIGHT-ARMED FRIEND?" DEMETER repeated up on Mount Olympus. She had been watching the humans carefully. "Sounds like we're about to get company, Zeus."

"One thing at a time." Zeus hurried to his food bowl and crammed a few nuggets of Fuzzy Feast into his mouth. "I need to figure out what Poseidon's up to."

"Poseidon?" Demeter repeated. "What about Poseidon?"

Zeus waved toward the suddenly supersize Aegean. "It's obvious he wanted to double his realm while I was cooped up."

Demeter walked to the edge of the palace, treading delicately in the portion that hung over the void, and scanned the Aegean Sea. It was really more of an ocean now, and she didn't see any sign of the pufferfish. "That doesn't sound like Poseidon, not after the adventures we've been on together lately." She walked back to Zeus, who was still stuffing Fuzzy Feast into his mouth.

Meanwhile, down in the pet center, Artie returned with two clear plastic bags full of water.

"Ooh! Those baggies hold an eight-armed friend?" Callie tried to inspect the bags' contents, but her view was distorted by the plastic.

"Yep! And then some!" Artie sounded giddy as she set the larger bag on the floor and untied the other one, upending it into the new tank. "May I introduce ... the Sirens!" Callie caught a glimpse of two sleek, slimy, snakelike creatures, each about a foot long with stubby legs.

"Sirens, huh? You mean like mermaids from the salty old sailing yarns?" She watched the animals disappear into the swaying grasses. "They don't look like mermaids."

Artie was already hefting the other plastic bag. "Now say hello to Proteus the mimic octopus."

Callie got only the faintest glimpse of a bulbous body surrounded by eight skinny legs that looked like striped jump ropes. In an instant, the octopus morphed into a fishlike creature, then into something resembling a stingray, before settling to the bottom of the tank, where it blended into the sand and disappeared.

"That was so cool." Callie was mesmerized.

"I know, right? Mimic octopuses are shape-shifters! They can change their color and texture to appear like all kinds of other sea creatures!"

"Where'd this one come from?" Callie asked.

"Well, originally, Egypt." Artie was dunking a cup to check the water quality. "They live in the Red Sea. This guy and his Siren buddies came from an enthusiastic aquarist who got in over his head."

"He's lucky he has you to take care of him." Callie scanned the bottom of the tank for any signs of the shape-shifting creature. "I take it the name Proteus is inspired by mythology?"

Artie smiled. Of course it was.

"I sure hope he gets along with your pufferfish," Callie said.

CHAPTER 5

UP ON MOUNT OLYMPUS, ZEUS AND
Demeter were so busy arguing about whether
Poseidon was behind the Aegean expansion,
they missed Artie's introduction of Greece's latest
residents.

"You and Poseidon have never gotten along better,"
Demeter implored. "You were even roommates!"

"Yeah, but not, like, willingly." Zeus sat on his
Golden Fleece bed and inspected his paws. "My fingers
get pruny just thinking about it."

"The team gets along so well now," Demeter pressed.
"We have so much ... mojo. It doesn't check out for him
to just make a power grab while you're stuck up here."

"Guess I'll know soon enough." Zeus hopped from

his bed and stood tall at the pillars of his palace, puffing out his chest. "My days of being stuck up here are over."

Suddenly, familiar harp music wafted up from the countryside. "The Oracle!" Demeter exclaimed.

Zeus's chest deflated as he found the source of the music: Artie was playing with the black rectangular device she carried with her everywhere. "It's kinda late for a lesson," he said.

The music softened as Artie stuck the device in her back pocket and began hastily cleaning up. The music faded as a voice began speaking: "Welcome to Greeking Out, your weekly podcast that delivers the goods on Greek gods and epic tales of triumphant heroes. I'm your host, the Oracle of Wi-Fi."

Zeus stared longingly at the rear door to his palace, then down to the Aegean. Freedom beckoned. "This is a waste of time!"

"I dunno, Zeus." Demeter settled in to listen and took a bite from her lettuce sash. "The Oracle has never wasted our time."

"This episode of Greeking Out is brought to you by the Samos Hamster System," the Oracle said. "If your hamster's sick of the same old, same old, send 'em scurrying through the Samos tunnels!"

"I'm sure sick of the same old, same old," Zeus muttered. His eyes were still locked on the back door.

"Hush! The Oracle will help us!" Demeter exclaimed.

"Today's tale is a doozy," the Oracle continued. "In fact, it's one of the most epic journeys of all time: the Odyssey."

"The Oddest Sea?" Zeus repeated, his ears perking up. "Maybe this won't be a waste of time after all."

"Told ya," Demeter whispered.

"Epic journeys are a common theme in Greek mythology," the Oracle explained. "Tales of mortal heroes undergoing fantastic voyages and defeating fearsome monsters with the help or hindrance of the gods. But all other adventures pale when compared to the voyage of Odysseus."

"Ol' Dizzy-us?" Zeus repeated, mangling the name.

"Oh-dis-ee-us," Demeter corrected.

"Odysseus was the king of the faraway land of Ithaca. He was a major player in a famous conflict known as the

Trojan War, which is a story for another time, faithful listeners."

"Awww," said Callie, who was restocking a rack with cat brushes that had fallen to the floor. "I would have loved to hear the tale of the Trojan War."

"The Oddest Sea!" Zeus demanded. "Get to the Oddest Sea!"

"This tale is set after the war," the Oracle continued, "when Odysseus boarded his ship bound for home. His journey was anything but smooth sailing. He lurched through storms and sought shelter on strange islands filled with fearsome beings, such as the one-eyed Cyclops. Sea monsters tracked down his vessel. In one narrow strait, he was forced to choose between an encounter with either Charybdis, a living whirlpool, or Scylla, a serpent with a bottomless appetite."

"I'd pick the one named Silly,'" Zeus offered.

"Sill-ah," Demeter corrected. "She pronounced it Sill-ah."

"Odysseus knew that Charybdis would swallow his entire ship, so he took his chances with Scylla. His crew hoisted every sail, hoping to zip out of tentacle range of the sea beast. They were fast, but not quite fast enough. Odysseus's vessel survived, but six of his sailors did not. They were snatched from the deck by the voracious monster."

Zeus's cheek patch twitched. "Nothing silly about Scylla."

"Eventually Odysseus and his crew entered the waters of the Sirens, beautiful but dangerous mermaid–like creatures whose songs lulled sailors into a relaxed, forgetful state. Odysseus's crew only survived by plugging their ears with wax."

"Eww." Zeus ran a finger around one of his ears.

"Good to know, though," Demeter added.

"Odysseus's odyssey brought him into contact with hundreds of colorful characters, from the great warrior Achilles to Proteus, a shape–changing creature who could predict the future."

Demeter's antennae perked up. "Maybe this Proteus character can tell us why the Aegean got all gigantic."

"I dunno," Zeus said. "My experience with these soothsaying types is that they're pretty stingy with information."

"But Proteus only foretold the future if he was lulled to sleep and captured," the Oracle explained.

"Yeah, see, there's always something," Zeus added.

"Odysseus never tracked down Proteus, but he came across other treats and treasures. And his voyage ended with the greatest prize of all," the Oracle continued.

Zeus's eyes widened.

"It took him a decade to reach it."

"Five years?!" Zeus hollered, incredulous.

"Ten years," Demeter corrected.

"Too long to listen to tonight." Artie tapped her black rectangle, stopping the Oracle mid-story. "It's well past closing time." She yawned and stretched her arms high as she surveyed all the fallen merchandise still strewn around the center. "I'll finish cleaning up tomorrow." She hurried around, scooping food into bowls, checking the animals, turning off lights.

"Oh my," said Callie, who was standing by the cash register. "Zeus is really living on the edge." She stood on her tippy-toes and slid the hamster's habitat back onto its shelf. Zeus stumbled as the palace floor shifted beneath him. His grin faded. The last thing he needed was for Artie or Callie to notice that his back door wasn't secure.

"Thanks. I'm glad you spotted that," Artie said, gathering her things. "It would kill me if Zeus got hurt—

even if he can be a stinker."

"It's more likely his house would break open and he'd escape. Speaking of which ..." She reached behind Zeus's habitat to make sure his back door was still secure. Zeus's stomach dropped as he watched her hand inch closer to the propped-up hatch.

CRUNCH! "Hey!" Callie's foot had crushed a piece of smashed plastic, which she bent down to examine. "The security system took a tumble."

"It's late. Let's go," Artie said. She was already standing at the front door. "Zeus can go unmonitored for one night. We'll get all this sorted out tomorrow."

The hamster beamed with relief.

Callie shoved the pieces of the security camera in her tool bag and joined Artie. She turned back to Zeus. "Funny," Callie said, as she stepped out the door into the night. "It almost looks like Zeus is smiling."

CHAPTER 6

THE OLYMPIANS WERE UNSUPERVISED FOR the first time in weeks. And Zeus was free.

Finally. He could resume his duties as king of the gods. More important, he could roam his realm once again. "Olympians, assemble!" From his vantage point on Mount Olympus, Zeus's voice boomed across Greece. He exalted as he watched Ares charge from his kennel with Hermes right behind, her speckled crown of short feathers flopping in all directions. Athena, not appearing quite as enthusiastic, rounded the shore of the Aegean Sea and trotted toward the meeting place.

"We're getting the gang together?" asked Demeter as she squeezed through the pillars of the palace and unfolded her wings.

"Almost." Zeus was watching the surface of the Aegean impatiently, waiting for Poseidon to emerge. His dive helmet, hoisted by his retinue of seahorses, should have risen already, yet Zeus saw no sign of it. "If you won't come to me, sea lord," Zeus muttered, "I guess I'll just have to come to you." He raced out the broken back door of his palace and spotted the string he used to descend from Mount Olympus. He leapt onto it and began scurrying down, but halfway to the ground he felt the string jerk. It was slipping from its tether! Zeus loosened his grip and let the string slide between his paws like a zip line, hoping he could ride down it before it collapsed.

His spiky hair billowed above his golden laurel crown as he gained speed. Just inches from the ground, the string came loose, sending Zeus into free fall.

He hit the ground and rolled, coming to a stop in a pile of coiled string.

He rubbed his sore paws and peered up at his palace. Now he had no way to get home. "That could've gone better." Just then he noticed a scruff of golden fur against the base of Mount Olympus. "Zeus Deuce!" Zeus grabbed his clone and heaved it over his shoulder. "Our adventures continue, good lookin'!" He took off at a run toward the Agora—and immediately ran into the edge of the Aegean Sea. "Blast it!" Zeus muttered.

"Over here, boss!" It was Ares's voice, not far off to the west. Zeus saw the pug along with Athena, Hermes, and Demeter all gathered in the Agora. The rope-wrapped pillars that formed their meeting place were no longer arranged in a neat circle. Artie hadn't paid much attention to setting them back up after the quake.

"Welcome back, *me*. I'm freeee!" Zeus strolled triumphantly between the Olympians. Ares danced excited circles around his king.

"Good to have ya back, Zeus." Hermes extended a white-speckled wing and bowed low. The silver chain around her chest—a gift from the Amazons—tinkled against the ground. "Things were gettin' a bit borin' around here."

"Not anymore." Zeus beamed, setting down Zeus Deuce. "Your prayers have been answered."

"Who would we pray to?" Ares tilted his head quizzically. "I mean, we're gods."

Zeus waved away the question. "And to think you all doubted Escape Plan Achilles."

Athena frowned. "I'm not sure your plan is what got you out. But in any case, we're all glad you're here—big things are afoot!"

Ares narrowed his eyes. "There's a big thing with a foot? Where?"

"Stand down, war god." Hermes patted Ares on his rump. "The big thing Athena is referrin' to is the Aegean Sea. Which is literally a big thing now. Er, a bigger thing."

Zeus crossed his arms. "Poseidon's got a lot of explaining to do."

"Why?" Hermes asked.

"He's in charge of the ocean," Zeus replied, his cheek patch quivering. I'm in charge of ... everything not the ocean." He waved his arms vaguely around Greece.

"Except the Underworld," Ares added. "Hades said he's in charge of the Underworld."

The other Olympians cringed. Zeus's expression went cold. His cheek patch was now roiling like a storm cloud.

Before he could reply, Athena stepped forward. "We're getting off track here. Let's just go find Poseidon and get to the bottom of this." She moved off in the direction of the seashore.

Zeus had regained his composure. "How will we get to the bottom of this when the answer's hidden at the bottom of that?" He waved toward the Aegean Sea. "But whatever." He took off after Athena. Ares, Hermes, and Demeter followed.

CHAPTER 7

AS SOON AS THE OLYMPIANS REACHED
the new shoreline of the Aegean, Zeus cupped
his paws around his mouth and hollered,
"Olympians, assemble!"

Ares immediately sprinted off into the distance, ran
in a large circle, then skidded to a halt in front of Zeus.
"Assembled!"

Zeus rolled his eyes. "Poseidon!" he yelled. "I said,
'Assemble!'"

When summoned in the past, the pufferfish had
always emerged from the sea in his dive helmet, which
was attached to his watery home with a long rubber
hose that provided him oxygen. The helmet allowed
him to travel with the land animals. This time, the sea's

surface—although rougher than usual—remained unbroken.

"Poseidon!" Zeus yelled again. Silence.

Zeus wrinkled his face in annoyance.

"He ever not show up before?" asked Hermes. She was the newest member of the Olympians.

"Never," Athena answered. "I mean, sometimes he'll show up reluctantly. But he always shows up."

"Humph," Zeus muttered.

"Zeus and Poseidon have had, uh, issues in the past," Demeter explained.

"Weren't you two roommates once?" Hermes asked.

"Why does everyone keep bringing that up?!" Zeus fumed. "He always comes when I call him. Until now, after his realm has conveniently doubled in size."

"There has to be some explanation." Athena padded to the water's edge and peered into the sea's depths. Usually the waters of the Aegean were clear, but now they were oddly churned up.

"Why's the water so cloudy?" asked Demeter.

"I dunno," Athena said. "The earthquake ended a while ago. The water should be back to normal by now."

"None of this feels normal," Demeter added.

"We have to go find Poseidon," Zeus declared.

"I agree," Athena replied. "He might be in trouble."

"He's the sea lord," Zeus shot back. "He can take care of himself. I think he's up to no good."

The other Olympians looked skeptical. They weren't convinced. Hermes broke the awkward silence. "How ya gonna find him?"

"The Oracle mentioned some know-it-all named Proteus," Zeus said. "I bet he could tell me where to find Poseidon—or at least why his realm suddenly got a whole lot bigger."

"The Oracle also mentioned something about the greatest prize of all," Demeter added. "Whatever that is, sounds handy!"

Hermes shook her head. "What I mean is, how you gonna find Poseidon—or Proteus, for that matter—in all of that?" She gestured toward the Aegean. "You don't seem like the type of god that can walk on water."

"Hermes is right. We'll need a seaworthy vessel," Athena mused. "I'm sure that I can adapt the *Argo* for ocean travel."

Zeus's face fell. "How long will that take?"

"I dunno." Athena's whiskers twitched in thought. "A couple of nights?"

"A couple of nights!" Zeus scoffed. "I barely have a couple of hours!"

"Why?" Demeter asked. "What's the rush?"

Zeus glanced up to Mount Olympus, remembering that he had no way to get home since the string had snapped. He ran a paw through his spiky hair above the golden laurel crown and decided not to mention it. "I ... uh." He shuffled his feet. "I'm just antsy is all."

"I'll work as fast as I can, Zeus," Athena said. "Ares, come assist me with the *Argo*—"

"No time for that!" Zeus exclaimed. "Demeter, come help me."

"Help you with what exactly?" The confused grasshopper asked.

"We need to build a boat!" Zeus said.

The other Olympians watched as Zeus and Demeter scrambled away.

CHAPTER 8

IT WASN'T LONG BEFORE ARES GREW
impatient and ran after Zeus and Demeter. "Let's
build a boat! Let's build a boat!" he yelled, charging
up behind them. They were scouring the hillside for
useful artifacts.

"We can't build a boat big enough for you, war god,"
Zeus answered. "But you could help us out another way."
Zeus had spotted Ares's bowl, which had already been
emptied of Mutt Nuggets. "Let me borrow your bowl!"

"Okay!" The pug charged away and grabbed his red
bowl, eager to help. "Whaffor?" he mumbled around the
bulky plastic in his mouth.

"For the boat! The body-thingy!" Zeus exclaimed.
"The part Demeter and I will sit in to drive the boat!"

Demeter considered the bowl skeptically. "I'm going with you?" she said.

"Of course!" Zeus clapped Demeter on the back. "Just you and me! Like old times!"

"It's called a hull," said Athena. She and Hermes had decided to join the group.

"Hull," Zeus repeated. "Right. I knew that."

"And you don't drive a boat," Athena added. "You sail it."

"Don't you drive the *Argo*?" Hermes asked.

"Well, that's different." Athena shook her head, jingling the owl charm on her collar. "The *Argo*'s a land vessel."

"How come you know so much about boats?" Demeter asked.

"I'm the goddess of wisdom—knowing stuff is my thing." Athena gave a big smile. "When boat builders need inspiration, they pray to *me!*"

Zeus bristled. "If you think I'm praying to you—"

"You'll also need a mast," Athena added quickly.

"Good thinking!" Zeus scanned the artifacts that scattered across Greece after the earthquake. "Mast ... mast ... If I were a mast, where and, uh ... what would I be?"

"Maybe you *should* pray to Athena," Hermes said.

Athena sighed. "A mast is like a tall pole. It holds up the sail."

Ares, uninterested in sailing terms, had dropped his food bowl and grasped the rubber bone he'd been chewing earlier between his two front paws. He was about to bite into it when—

"That'll make a great mast!" Zeus plucked the bone away. "Nice find, Ares!"

The pug watched Zeus drag the bone and drop it in his food bowl. "Thanks?"

"So next we need a sail," Demeter said, scanning the littered ground around her. "Sail, sail, sail ..."

Ares shuffled a few feet away and scooped up a round white disc the size of a dinner plate. The top of the disc bore bold dayglow markings above a smaller script in a foreign language.

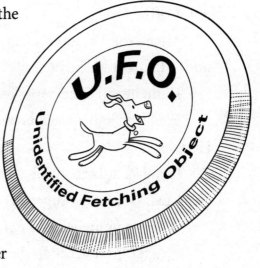

"This is boring!" Ares complained, prodding the disc with his wrinkly nose. "Hermes, let's play! Catch!" Ares scooped up the disc in his mouth and whipped it at Hermes with a jerk of his neck. The disc spun as it flew in a tight arc, straight toward Hermes's head.

"The perfect sail!" Athena cried. She leapt in front of Hermes and batted the disc toward Zeus.

"Eeek!" Zeus leapt over the disc as it clattered to a stop near the bowl and bone. "Hey," he said, appreciating the pile of parts. "We've got everything we need to build our boat!"

"Ah-ah-ah." Hermes raised a wing. "Almost. You still need a figurehead. All boats need a figurehead."

"Figurehead?" Demeter asked.

"Wait, you know about boats, too?" Ares asked Hermes.

"I know a little about a lot of things," Hermes answered. "Especially superstitious stuff."

"What's a figurehead?" Zeus interrupted impatiently.

"It's a figure attached to the front of a boat," Hermes explained.

"I don't have time for that," Zeus snapped.

"Why do we need a figurehead?" Demeter asked.

"It's bad luck to sail without one," Hermes said. "Without a figurehead, your ship is doomed."

"Zeus, we need a figurehead," Demeter said flatly.

"Fine." Zeus fumed, but then his face brightened. "Good thing we already have one!"

CHAPTER 9

THE OLYMPIANS GATHERED AT THE WATER'S edge, next to Zeus's newly assembled boat. He was busy stowing Fuzzy Feast and extra lettuce bits for his and Demeter's voyage on the Oddest Sea. The boat's shiny hull glowed a deep crimson in the red light cast by the Mount Olympus Pet Center sign. The disc-shaped sail was lowered face down on its rubber-bone mast, ready for hoisting. Zeus Deuce had been drafted to be the figurehead and was strapped upright at the bow of the ship.

Hermes inspected the finished product and whistled. "For such a mangy ball of fluff, ol' Zeus Deuce makes a pretty good figurehead."

"The best figurehead," Zeus said absentmindedly as

he swept the last few crumbs of Ares's Mutt Nuggets from the bottom of the hull, then buffed out a spot of slobber.

Beside the boat, Athena and Ares had just finished leaning two long, clear plastic tunnels—raided from Artie's new collection of tubes—against the steep shoreline of the Aegean Sea. The tubes would serve as a ramp to launch the boat into the water.

Hermes positioned the boat at the bottom of the ramp. Around the hull she wrapped a long string, which she ran to the top of the ramp and back to its base to help launch the vessel. Zeus and Demeter hopped aboard and arranged the lines they would use to raise the sail.

Meanwhile, Athena paced nervously along the shoreline. "I really advise you to put this adventure off for just a night or two," she said, "until I can adapt the *Argo* and we can all go."

Zeus's cheek patch quivered. He seemed ready to argue, but then his expression softened. "I appreciate you lookin' out for me," he said, "but remember, I'm the king of the gods. There's nothing I can't handle."

"Oh, I can think of a few things you couldn't handle," Athena replied. "Charybdis, for instance."

"And the Minotaur!" Ares added helpfully. "Don't forget the Minotaur!"

"And the Hydra—" Hermes offered.

"I get it!" Zeus cut them off.

"The point is," Athena hastily continued, "we're at our best when we're together."

"I know—we all know—we got mojo," Zeus admitted, "but you guys all got to go on the last adventure without me. And I've been cooped up too long." He gazed longingly out to sea. "I need to stretch my legs—I need this adventure!" The excitement in his voice was obvious.

Athena looked at Demeter for help, but the grasshopper just shrugged.

"Okay," Athena said, "but can we at least agree to rendezvous? Say, at midnight?"

"Sure, midnight," Zeus said impatiently. He picked up the string Hermes had run from the boat to the top of the ramp and tossed its end to Ares, who grabbed it with his mouth.

"Where will we meet?" Demeter asked.

"On Crete," Athena said. "Let's meet on Crete."

"Crete, sure, you bet." Zeus was hardly paying attention. "Okay, war god, heave!"

Ares tugged at the string. It pulled taut and then slowly began hauling the boat up to the water's edge.

"Wait!" Hermes cried. "Hold on! You haven't named yer boat yet!"

"What's it need a name for?" Zeus sounded annoyed. They inched closer to the water as Ares continued to pull the string.

"Are names good luck, too?" Demeter asked.

"Yep!" Hermes replied.

Zeus sighed. "Fine. How about we call it ..." He scratched his chin. "The *Argo 2!*"

Athena wrinkled her nose. "Hmm, I don't know about that. Sounds awfully ... grandiose."

The boat was halfway up the ramp. "I take it you have a better name in mind?" Zeus demanded.

Athena watched the small craft inch closer to the water's edge. "How about ... the *Argo ½?*"

"Fine, whatever," Zeus snapped. The hull tipped over

the top of the ramp and—*SPLISH!*—landed in the water. It teetered but settled on the wavy surface of the Aegean.

Zeus untied the launch string from the hull and let Hermes coil it back on shore. "Hoist the main sail!" he commanded.

Demeter looked around the cramped hull. "We only have one sail."

"Hoist that one then!"

Demeter tugged at the lines with all her strength, but the sail didn't budge. "A little help?" she asked.

Zeus rushed to her side and heaved on the rigging. Together they pulled the mast upright, locking it in place against the hull. The disc-shaped sail caught the soft breeze. Zeus and Demeter cruised smoothly away as the Olympians waved goodbye from onshore.

"Remember, rendezvous at midnight!" Athena called. "On Crete!"

Zeus didn't answer. The *Argo ½* was sailing away on the Oddest Sea.

CHAPTER 10

DEMETER STOOD AT THE BOW OF THE
Argo ½, enjoying the breeze blowing against her
antennae. "You know, sailing is kinda fun—pttt,
blah, blech." A strand of golden hair had caught in her
mouth. Demeter realized with disgust it was from the
ratty hide of Zeus Deuce, their figurehead.

"Of course it's fun, when you have me as the
captain." Zeus stood tall at the rigging, letting the
breeze muss his spiky hair. "Whoa!" The boat suddenly
leaned hard to the left. Zeus heaved on a line and
twisted the sail. The deck leveled out below their feet.
Zeus whooped. "I'm a natural at this," he said, "if I do
say so myself."

"I *don't* say so myself," Demeter muttered as she

clutched her belly. Her stomach had started doing somersaults since they'd reached deeper waters. Although Zeus had figured out how to set the sail just right to catch the breeze, the *Argo ½* was constantly zigging and zagging, jibing and tacking, leaning to and fro.

Demeter tried to keep her mind off her topsy-turvy stomach. She could see all the way down to the sandy bottom of the Aegean Sea far below, despite the slight cloudiness in the seawater. They passed over gardens of coral and forests of seaweed. The occasional tropical fish—each a riot of rainbow-colored scales—darted by. "Poseidon's realm is stunning," Demeter mused.

"Sure," Zeus admitted as he heaved on the rigging yet again. The boat lurched across the wind and settled into a new tack. "I mean, as long as I'm riding above it rather than in it, and not getting my paws all pruny—pffft, blah, blah." He spat out a strand of Zeus Deuce's mane.

"I think our figurehead is shedding," Demeter said.

"It happens." Zeus brushed the loose fur off his cheek patch with one paw, then nearly flopped to the deck as the sail jerked the line in his other paw. "The wind's picking up."

Demeter climbed up the mast and perched near the top, holding on with four legs in the stiffening breeze. The sea around them had gone from mildly choppy to rolling swells.

Within moments, the waves gave way to foamy whitecaps that crashed around them. Demeter shielded her eyes with a leg and peered into the distance, where the seas were churning even more. "I ... think we're sailing into a storm," Demeter hollered down to Zeus.

"Which way should we go?!" Zeus grappled with the line, trying to change course again. Waves were beginning to break over the side of the boat. Zeus Deuce's fur was a sopping mop. Zeus felt something mushy at his feet and looked down to find a waterlogged crumb of Fuzzy Feast in the seawater puddling at the boat's bottom. The boat lurched again, and he immediately returned his attention to the dark horizon.

Demeter scrambled as high as she dared on the mast, practically standing on it, and scanned in all directions for any sign of calmer seas. "We should probably turn around and head back to—What was that?!" A dark flicker had caught her attention—just the briefest glimpse of a black slimy body breaking the surface not far ahead. Demeter called down, "Zeus? I don't think we're alone out here!"

CHAPTER 11

ZEUS, BUSY HANDLING THE ARGO ½ IN THE growing storm, failed to heed Demeter's warning. He wrestled with the rigging while standing in water up to his ankles.

Demeter hopped from the mast, her seasickness forgotten, and began bailing out the boat. Yet no matter how fast she bailed, she couldn't keep ahead of the waves crashing over the side. "Zeus, we're taking on too much water! Help!"

"I can't! I have to hold our course in this wind!" he shouted as the sack of waterlogged Fuzzy Feast slid into him, nearly knocking him down.

Suddenly, the *Argo* ½ lurched to the left, throwing Zeus and Demeter to the deck. Zeus scrambled to his feet—the water was up to his knees now—then froze. He saw a massive black body, shiny with slime, sliding underneath the boat, almost as if it was trying to lift them out of the water. "We're not alone out here!" he yelled.

"That's what I just—" Demeter stopped short when she saw Zeus backing away from an enormous thick, black, slimy, noodle-like *thing*—the same thing she had spotted from the mast. It was some sort of tentacle, covered with serrated suckers. Whatever monster this tentacle was attached to—Demeter shuddered to imagine such a creature—it obviously had no problem keeping pace in the depths below. "It's Scylla," Demeter said in a low voice. "The monster from the Oracle's lesson. It has to be."

"Okay, yeah, we should turn back." Zeus sloshed across the flooded deck and grabbed the line that controlled the sail.

Demeter watched as the slimy tentacle arched over the *Argo ½*, preparing to wrap it in a crushing embrace. "We can't outrun it, Zeus!"

"No, but we can outmaneuver it!" Zeus wrapped the

line around his forearm several times, then yanked, bringing the *Argo ½* fully about. It skidded in a half circle into the eye of the wind, abruptly stalling. Zeus and Demeter stumbled through waist-deep water toward the stern as Scylla's tentacle came crashing down, missing the boat by a hair's width. Foamy seawater cascaded over the stern, filling the already swamped hull.

"You really are a natural at this." Demeter's mouth hung open in amazement as she watched Scylla's tentacle thrash behind the boat.

Zeus took a bow. "Told ya," he said. Behind him, the trunk-like tentacle re-emerged, reaching for the sky, rigid as a tree. Demeter stared at the towering appendage. Zeus saw the fear in her eyes and turned to see Scylla poised above the *Argo ½*.

"Eek!" He yanked the rigging hard again, trying to adjust the sail and get them moving. His efforts were fruitless. The sail was bent backward and didn't respond to his tugging. The wind was pushing the boat in reverse—directly toward Scylla.

BUMP. They both jumped as the boat's stern made

contact with the slimy tentacle. Scylla arched its tentacle downward, its slimy tip homing in on Zeus's head. "Do something," Demeter said urgently. "Do that outmaneuver thing again!"

Zeus gave one last tug on the sail. "Ungh!" The white disc broke away from the mast. Zeus splashed onto the flooded deck, where the sail fell over him. Instead of grabbing Zeus, Scylla's tentacle latched onto the sail and hurled it high into the sky, away from the *Argo ½*. The disc landed amid turbulent waves and spun strangely upright for a moment, like a giant spinning coin on the sea. Then another gust caught it and the sail skipped off. The motion must have attracted Scylla. The massive tentacle retracted and raced off after the sail.

Zeus and Demeter watched the monster fade into the distance as the sea raged around them. "Well," Zeus said, "we did better than Ol' Dizzy-us or whatever his name was. He lost six crew members to Scylla." He motioned down to the swamped hull of the *Argo ½*. "We just lost our sail."

Demeter was shocked at how badly the *Argo ½* had flooded. The boat floated low in the churning seas.

Its deck looked like a swimming pool, and storm waves continued to wash over the side. "I think we lost more than the sail, Zeus," she said, hopping atop the mast to get above the waterlogged hull. "We're sinking."

"Sinking?" Zeus flicked at the water lapping at his chest. "This is just a puddle. We can bail it out." He cupped his paws to scoop out a handful of seawater, but as he did, the boat suddenly plunged into the sea beneath him, leaving his feet with no deck to stand on. He sank up to his neck and began treading water furiously to stay afloat.

Demeter rode the sinking mast until her legs hit the water. She released her grip on the rubber bone as it plunged into the murky depths.

The *Argo* ½ had sunk. Zeus and Demeter bobbed in a raging ocean, with a sea monster lurking nearby.

CHAPTER 12

ZEUS TREADED FURIOUSLY TO KEEP HIS head above the storm-tossed waves. Demeter could practically walk on the water, but the raging sea kept threatening to toss her on her back.

"We're in trouble, Zeus!" Demeter yelled into the howling wind.

"No kidding!" Zeus spat seawater, then held up a paw and wriggled his wrinkled paws. "I don't think I've ever been this pruny."

"We're land animals! Do you see land?" Demeter gestured around her wildly. "Because I don't!"

"Ahh, you're overreacting." Zeus shrugged, but then slipped underwater for a moment before sputtering to the surface. "Storms, sea monsters—these sorts of things were all part of that Ol' Dizzy-us guy's journey on the Oddest Sea, remember? That's what the Oracle said, anyway." He waved around approvingly. "Things are all going according to plan."

"According to plan?!" Demeter raged. "ACCORDING TO WHOSE PLAN?! I mean, Hades couldn't come up with a better plan if he wanted to get rid of us for good!"

"Just go with the flow, buddy." Zeus tried to float on his back. "Everything will work out." A wave flipped him over. He wiped his hair from his eyes and resumed treading water.

SPLISH! Something broke the surface behind them. Demeter turned slowly, expecting to see a slimy black tentacle. Zeus kicked himself higher for a better view. Both were shocked to see three golden tines rising slowly out of the water. It was a trident, wielded by a spotted pufferfish wearing a golden crown.

"Poseidon!" Demeter exclaimed. "Are we glad to see you!" She stumbled as whitecaps frothed around her legs, then recovered. "Did you see the sea monster?!"

"Where have you been?" Zeus demanded.

Poseidon didn't respond. He floated gracefully in the

roiling water, eyeing Demeter and Zeus with a strange expression. He wasn't in his dive helmet, of course—he only needed that to travel on land among the air-breathing Olympians.

Zeus shouted at Poseidon, "I asked you a question!"

The pufferfish laughed—a deep, raspy laugh, like wind through a pile of dead leaves. Zeus had never heard that laugh before. Poseidon's oversize eyes didn't even blink.

"What's so funny?!" Zeus yelled. Another wave crashed on his head. Zeus reappeared a moment later, treading frantically. "Never mind," he sputtered, shaking water from the spiky fur on his head. "Just push us to shore."

Without a word, Poseidon sank beneath the waves until only the tip of his crown was visible. He swam slowly toward Zeus, the crown cutting through the waves like the dorsal fin of a shark. "The sea lord picked the wrong day to ride my last nerve," Zeus growled to Demeter.

"I dunno," Demeter replied. "Something is off about him."

"YOWW!" Zeus nearly leapt out of the water when Poseidon prodded him with his trident from below. "Don't push us with your silly sea fork!" he shouted into the water.

Poseidon broke the surface again. His eyes were narrow slits. "You dare give me orders in my own realm?" His voice was as cold as his expression.

Demeter tilted her head quizzically. Something about Poseidon's voice—its tone—seemed wrong. It sounded like it was slower and an octave lower than usual.

"Don't start with the power trip stuff now," Zeus warned. "You already have a lot of explaining to do."

Poseidon slipped beneath the waves again. For a moment, Demeter caught a glimpse of ... *something* in the depths beneath the sea lord—something striped and fluttering—but then she felt Poseidon's trident press against her side. "OUCH!" She grabbed the cold tines with two legs and lurched into motion as Poseidon began pulling her through the water. "Hey, grab on!" She reached out her other legs so Zeus could hitch a ride.

They raced through the water. Zeus could see Poseidon's crown cutting through the surface. "At least Poseidon is giving us a lift."

"Yeah, but in the wrong direction!" Demeter saw with alarm that they were heading farther out to sea, into rougher waters.

"Hey, fish face!" Zeus kicked underwater at Poseidon and made contact with his crown. The pufferfish rose to the surface, his expression sour. "You're taking us the wrong way!" Zeus yelled.

"Wrong," Poseidon replied in his odd voice. Then he laughed that deep, rumbling laugh again. "I'm taking you in precisely the correct direction."

"Where?!" Demeter braced herself as another wave washed across them.

"To your watery grave," Poseidon said matter-of-factly. He gave the duo one final push into a current that dragged them straight out to sea.

Zeus and Demeter watched Poseidon sink beneath

the whitecaps. "There! There it is again!" She'd seen the striped *somethings*—tentacles, maybe—fluttering in the depths where Poseidon had been.

"There *what* is again?" Zeus asked, trying to follow Demeter's pointing leg. The current was carrying them fast and far. A heavy wave crashed down, pushing Zeus under and separating him from Demeter. Zeus pumped his arms and legs only to realize he'd gotten disoriented and was actually swimming downward. He could see Demeter gliding on the waves above him. He kicked to the surface for a gulp of air—only to be driven under by another wave. He got a lungful of foamy seawater and coughed and sputtered.

Sinking, sinking, Zeus was running out of strength; his eyes stung from the seawater. Demeter was diving toward him, a front leg outstretched. He should have felt panicked—terrified at the idea of them both drowning. Instead, his last thought, before his vision went black, was that they would be late for their rendezvous with the Olympians.

CHAPTER 13

"**THEY'RE LATE**," HERMES SAID, SCANNING the shoreline of Crete.

"Of course they're late." Athena paced along the water. Hackles of gray fur stood along her back. "I didn't expect Zeus to be on time—that's not his style."

"But they're, like, super late," exclaimed Ares as he sniffed at a crate of artifacts nearby. "Like, super-duper late. Like, super-duper-duper—"

"Okay, got it." Athena cut him off.

The group had gathered on this small spit of land surrounded by the Aegean Sea to meet Zeus and Demeter. It was way past midnight.

"What'll we do if they don't show?" Hermes asked.

"We'll go find them," Athena said confidently.

"Y'all know I'm not a seabird." Hermes craned her neck to scan the vast sea, which was hard to take in past the high dunes that lined the shore.

"Where is Poseidon when we need him?" Athena flattened her fluffy ears. "We Olympians always work better together."

Splish-splish-SPLISH!

"You all hear that?" Ares stopped pacing and tilted his head.

Suddenly, a white disc came skipping over the sea's surface. "Ares, fetch!" Athena pointed at the object. The war god leapt, twisting in the air, and caught the disc in his mouth.

"Atta boy!" Hermes exclaimed.

Ares trotted to the other Olympians and dropped it at their feet. "Again! Again!" Ares shouted, his corkscrew tail wiggling. "Hermes, throw it to me!"

"Not now," Athena said. She was examining the disc Ares had fetched. She recognized it as the sail of the *Argo ½*. "Olympians, time for a rescue mission."

CHAPTER 14

ZEUS AWOKE WITH A START, SUCKED IN A
breath, and—*BLAARGH*—hacked up seawater.
He coughed and coughed, propped up on an
elbow. When his lungs finally cleared, he took in a
deep breath, almost expecting a mouthful of seawater.
Instead, he inhaled air! It was musty and had a strange,
canned quality, but to Zeus it was like taking a hearty
breath in a spring meadow. Had he dreamed the whole
misadventure on the Oddest Sea? Where was he?

Slowly his surroundings swam into focus. He was
in some type of clear sphere, like a hard-shelled bubble.
It was lit by a pulsing red glow that danced on the walls.
He hadn't dreamed his misadventure after all.

"Where am I?" he asked, shaking off the cobwebs.

His voice sounded hollow in the tight space.

"Bottom of the Oddest Sea, as near as I can tell," came Demeter's voice behind him. Zeus spun, spraying water from his soggy fur. Demeter stood a few inches away inside the bubble, toweling dry with a scrap of cloth. "You want this?" Demeter offered Zeus the sopping rag, but he ignored it. He stood at the wall, transfixed by what he saw. Demeter's cloth fell to the floor with a wet splat.

Zeus could just make out the sandy bottom of the Aegean. It extended around them outside the sphere, lit dimly from the ocean's surface far above. He took in stalks of tall plants bending in a fierce current.

They were in a seaweed grove, which made it hard to
see much in any direction. At the top of the sphere,
Zeus spotted rope netting that seemed to be holding the
bubble to the bottom, along with a black hose trailing
off into the distance. It burped the occasional bubble
that rose toward the red gloom of the surface. He heard
a faint hiss of air. "Wait a minute," Zeus said. "This place
feels really familiar."

"I should certainly hope so," came a muffled but
familiar voice. "You've been in there before." *TAP! TAP!
TAP!* Zeus spun around. There, hovering just outside
the sphere, was a spotted pufferfish. He was tapping the
outer wall with his trident.

"You!" Zeus roared. He leapt forward in anger until he was pressing against the curved inner wall of the bubble.

"Of course it's me," Poseidon said, puffing up with indignation. "Not exactly a grateful greeting for the Olympian who just saved your soggy hide."

"Saved us!" Zeus spat. "You're the reason we're here!" Zeus slapped the wall of the sphere, startling a jet-black seahorse hovering nearby.

"Easy, Arion, easy," Poseidon cooed to the leader of his seahorse team, calming him immediately. Arion and three other seahorses each wore harnesses attached to the hammock-like netting that held their sea lord's air-filled helmet in place.

"How could you, Poseidon?" Demeter said in a hurt tone. "After all our adventures together?"

"How could I *what*?" Poseidon deflated. He let his trident droop by his side. Arion and the other seahorses exchanged confused glances.

"Oh, I dunno," Zeus said, waving an arm angrily at his rear. "For starters, how could you jab me in the backside with your pitchfork?"

"And how could you push us out to sea? And then leave us to drown?" Demeter followed up, sounding nearly as angry as Zeus.

"What are the two of you talking about? I assure you I have neither jabbed nor pushed anyone anywhere today," Poseidon said. "You're lucky I found you at all. You have Arion to thank for that."

The black seahorse puffed out his chest proudly.

"Arion was following that rascal Proteus," Poseidon explained, "but when he saw you sinking into the drink, he came and got me."

"Proteus?" Demeter's antenna perked up. "Zeus, that's the guy we're searching for! The know-it-all who can help you find Poseidon!"

"Find me?" Poseidon narrowed his eyes. "I'm right here! And don't think you'd get any help from that shape-shifting fiend."

Zeus crossed his arms. "Quit trying to change the subject!"

"I'm in the same boat as you," Poseidon explained. "Well, almost." He motioned his trident at his dive helmet with Zeus and Demeter inside it. "Proteus can change appearance. He can make himself look like anyone. He did it to me. He took on my shape, crown, trident—the whole Poseidon package—and usurped me as sea lord." Poseidon raised a fin with realization. "It wasn't me who sent you out to sea. It was Proteus!"

"Says you!" Zeus snapped.

"How do we know *you're* not Proteus?" Demeter asked softly.

Poseidon rolled his eyes. "Because I just saved you from certain drowning."

"That checks out." Demeter nodded, then rubbed her chin thoughtfully. "And there was something odd about the Poseidon who pushed us out to sea—I could've sworn I saw a flash of tentacles."

"I don't have tentacles," Poseidon confirmed, wiggling his fins.

Zeus scoffed. "So let me get this straight. You're saying this Proteus guy somehow bested you, the sea lord, on your home turf."

Poseidon further deflated in a sputter of bubbles. "He does have a pet sea monster," the pufferfish said sheepishly.

"Scylla!" Demeter said. "We met it. It tried to sink our boat."

"Tried? I'd say it succeeded." Poseidon paused. "You know, Proteus has other minions to help him: a pair of Sirens. They sing a song that is just so ..." Poseidon's expression turned wistful. "... relaxing." He shook his head. "Anyway, my own minions here"—he waved toward the seahorses—"recognized that I was falling under the Sirens' spell. They are immune to the song and can block it out with their own special singing. So they whisked me away before the Sirens got too close and their song overpowered me."

As if on cue, Arion uttered a low growl, releasing a stream of bubbles. His body seemed to vibrate in time with the sound. The other seahorses joined in, creating a chorus of rumbling growls that only faded when the seahorses halted their singing.

Zeus smiled at Arion appreciably. "Hard to find good minions these days."

Arion turned up his nose with a snort, uttering an especially guttural growl.

"We're lucky you found us when you did," Demeter said. "Otherwise we would be sleeping with the fishes."

Poseidon swam up to peek above the top of the seaweed grove, searching for any sign of Proteus and his cronies. "I suppose I'm fortunate, too," he said. "You can help me kick Proteus off my throne and win back my kingdom."

Zeus's skeptical mood evaporated. "Right. Of course." He stood tall and squared his shoulders, puffing out the thunderbolt emblem on his chest. "I figured you would need my help. Well, it's all in a day's work for the king of the gods. I'm more than happy to save—"

"Um, Zeus," Demeter interrupted. "Don't you think we should assemble the team for this? Not that I doubt you can handle it," she added hastily. "It's just that we're kinda out of our element. Literally." She waved at the gloomy depths.

Zeus thought for a moment, then nodded. "We

Olympians do work better as a team. Which way to Crete?" he asked Poseidon.

"It's that way," he said, pointing east, "as the flying fish flies. But it would take you much too long to walk across the seafloor in my helmet."

"Well, the *Argo ½* should be on the bottom somewhere near here. Let's get her shipshape so we can sail to the meeting and get the others on board!"

"The *Argo ½*? Is that what you call your ... boat? Last I saw it, the vessel was sinking this way." Poseidon swam to the north. His seahorse team followed, pulling the dive helmet against the seafloor. Zeus and Demeter walked along as the sphere rotated jerkily around them. For Zeus this felt natural, like running on his wheel, but Demeter stumbled a few times before she got the hang of it.

The soggy towel Demeter had used to dry off slid around the floor, leaving a wet trail. Demeter stepped over it with her front legs but then caught a rear leg on it, sending her stumbling again.

"I miss riding on the *Argo ½*," she said as they entered the thick seaweed forest.

CHAPTER 15

BACK ON SHORE, THE ORIGINAL ARGO WAS in pieces. Ares had dismantled it, using his powerful jaws to rip open the vessel's underbelly and yank out its innards. In less than a minute, he had cleaned out its shell, leaving a hollow, tire-shaped hull topped with a flat deck. The vessel's internal components—wires, wheels, mechanisms—were strewn along the shoreline and covered with dog slobber. His head high, Ares spat out a cracked circuit board and turned to Athena, who had been watching him tear apart her vessel.

She smiled broadly. "Good god!"

Ares spun rapidly in circles, his Spartan war helmet teetering wildly.

Hermes walked up to the scene dragging a long-handled artifact with rows of teeth as well as two long, identical skinny artifacts emblazoned with strange markings. She took in the wreckage of the *Argo* and whistled. "Remind me never to get on your bad side, Ares buddy. You plucked out that thing's insides in two shakes."

Athena noticed the first orange fingers of sunlight creeping across Greece. "Two shakes might have been too long—we need to finish our modifications and set sail right away!"

The hen pointed at the two artifacts with strange markings she had found. "Will these work as oars?"

Athena took in the long rubber sticks, each topped with deep scoops. "Perfect!"

"And I got ya the ... whatchamacallit?" Hermes pointed at the artifact with teeth.

"The tiller! That'll do! Let's get these secured to the deck!"

Hermes—at Athena's direction—lashed the two rubber oars to either side of the *Argo*'s hull while the artifact with teeth trailed off the stern, its end dropping low to act as a rudder. Athena nodded approvingly at their handiwork. The *Argo* didn't look much different than when it was a land vessel—except for the addition of the oars and tiller. But the once-glowing crystals and buttons on the deck no longer functioned, and the hull was now a hollow shell—which was the goal. That meant it should float. "Seems seaworthy to me." Athena nodded. "Prepare to launch!"

Ares pushed the *Argo* against the base of the two clear plastic tube-shaped tunnels they had used as a ramp to launch the *Argo ½*, although this vessel was much larger and heavier. Ares took three steps back,

sank low, then rammed his Spartan war helmet full strength into the *Argo*, pushing it up the ramp. His stocky legs bulged as he shoved the vessel toward the top of the ramp. He had to stand on his hind legs and stretch his meatloaf-shaped body, but finally—with one strong hop and a grunt—he shoved the *Argo* over the edge and into the foaming sea.

"Launched!" Ares sat, panting hard.

Hermes and Athena held their breath as the *Argo* listed dangerously to one side. But then she righted herself and sat bobbing slightly in the waves.

"All aboard, Olympians!" Athena called. She ran gracefully up one of the tubes and landed softly on the *Argo*'s deck, one paw already on the tiller. Hermes fluttered after her, clawing at the air with her wings. She landed hard on their new boat's deck.

Hermes peered down at Ares on shore. "Wait, how's the war god gonna climb aboard?" she asked.

"Unfortunately, he's not," Athena replied in a low voice as she made sure the oars were secured to the deck. "Ares never rode aboard the *Argo* on land. He's not about to start now that we're on water."

"I can hear you over there!" Ares shouted at Athena. "No way you're leaving me behind!" His fatigue from launching the *Argo* forgotten, Ares leapt onto a crate near the shore of the Aegean, then clambered onto another one. "I've been working on my balance in my obstacle course!" he said, preparing for a final leap to board the *Argo*.

"Not sure that would help your sea legs," Athena yelled, panicked.

"Aw, let the big guy try." Hermes grinned.

Athena's reply was cut off by a low wail wafting through the air, just barely audible.

The sound froze the Olympians in place. It was strangely hypnotic. The wail slowly grew louder, evolving into angelic singing. One voice, then two created a haunting harmony. The notes soared to unearthly heights before dropping to earthshaking lows.

Athena and Ares were captivated, the rescue mission forgotten. Their eyelids

became heavy. Both cared only about listening to that song, that beautiful song. Athena curled up on the deck of the *Argo*. Ares sat down so hard, he tumbled from the top of the crate onto the shore, his feet in the air, mouth slack. He wanted the music to wash over him forever.

"What's the matter with y'all?!" Hermes cried.

To Athena, Hermes's voice sounded as if it was a great distance away. She didn't respond. She was annoyed that Hermes was distracting her from the magical melody.

"Snap out of it! Athena! Ares! Y'all, we got a job to do!" Hermes was now shouting. Athena and Ares remained in their dreamy state.

Suddenly the music faded.

Athena's eyes drifted open to find Hermes waving her wings frantically in front of her. On the beach, Ares was struggling to his feet, his tongue lolling out of his mouth.

"What ... what happened?" Athena asked, shaking the fog from her head.

"Heck if I know," Hermes responded. "Y'all just shut down. Gave up. It was like back in the Underworld, when Hypnos was doing his crazy eye thing."

"It was that music," Ares muttered, dripping slobber. He'd climbed back up on the crate and was limbering up to leap to the *Argo*. "It was just so ..."

"Relaxing," Athena said, finishing his thought. "Didn't you hear it?"

"Course I did." Hermes crossed her arms. "But I'm the goddess of sleep, among other things, remember? I'm immune to all that hypnosis stuff."

"Lucky," Ares said, still dazed. "Wish we were." Without warning, he hopped from the crate to the *Argo*'s deck. The vessel sank low in the water, waves washing over her. Athena and Hermes both tensed, ready to abandon ship, but then the vessel settled and rose high, as steady as when she was on land.

Athena relaxed and got back to prepping the *Argo*. "It could be a real problem if we run into that music again out at sea."

Hermes scratched thoughtfully at the rubbery red waddle under her chin, then reached up to her crest of short, wobbly feathers and plucked a few. "Take these," she said, holding out the feathers to Athena and Ares.

"What for?" Ares asked as he and Athena dutifully grabbed the short feathers.

"Remember how the Oracle said Odysseus's crew crammed wax in their ears to block the songs of those Sirens?" She wrinkled her face. "I figure a few feathers from the goddess of sleep would do the same job—and be a lot less gross."

Athena and Ares shrugged and stowed the feathers under their respective collars.

When Athena saw brighter rays of sunlight peeking across Greece, she said, "To the oars!" Hermes and Ares looked at each other, then each took up an oar—Hermes with her wings and Ares with his mouth. "Heave!" Athena commanded.

"Ho!" they both said as they began paddling. Hermes's chain jangled against her chest with each stroke. The *Argo* lurched forward and spun in a circle until Hermes and Ares coordinated their rowing.

"I feel like we're forgetting something," Hermes said as she pulled in unison with Ares.

"Too late," Athena muttered at the brightening sky. "We're too late."

CHAPTER 16

OSEIDON'S SEAHORSES HAULED THEIR
king's dive helmet across the bottom of the
Aegean, darting from cover to cover and
spending as little time on the open seafloor—in sight
of other fish—as possible. Poseidon, the true ruler of
this underwater realm, normally had nothing to fear
from his aquatic subjects. But Proteus could assume
the appearance of any creature. The Olympians couldn't
trust anyone.

The helmet's netting occasionally slipped and sent
Zeus and Demeter tumbling inside. They struggled
to keep up with the seahorses' pace and the helmet's
breakneck spin.

The wave-tossing storm had left the water cloudy.

Faint early morning light filtering from above ended in a foreboding gloom at the edge of their vision. It was as though they were socked in by a fog.

Zeus scanned for the wreckage of the *Argo ½*. His pulse quickened each time a new shape loomed out of the gloom. A menacing tangle of horns—like the antlers of a giant sea beast—turned out to be a towering coral structure, bordered by fans of swaying pink filaments.

Zeus breathed a sigh of relief, but he knew Scylla was out there, cruising the depths, just waiting for some tasty land animals to thrash, squish, and swallow.

"No shame in being jumpy, Zeus," Demeter said as they rolled through the coral garden. She had seen his reaction. "It's scary down here."

"I'm not scared!" Zeus snapped, never moving his eyes from the massive sandcastle they were passing. Bubbles percolated from its cavernous gatehouse. Who knew what strange creature lived inside.

"I'm not saying you're scared." Demeter was also staring at the castle. "It's just that this realm messes with your senses. I don't know how Poseidon lives down here without losing his noodle."

"I feel the same when I travel in your land realm."
Poseidon was keeping pace nearby.

"I have to say, Poseidon," Demeter said, "I have a newfound appreciation for how you get around on land in this thing. It is exhausting!"

"It's not so bad—" Zeus tumbled as the seahorses pulled the helmet to a sudden halt in the shadow of a seamount of jet-black rock.

"Hush now." Poseidon's voice dropped to a whisper. "We've arrived. This is Santorini. An underwater mountain, a seamount, formed long ago from the same powerful forces that created the world." He waved toward the mountain. "It's home to a special place." He paused, as if deciding whether to say more. Finally, he added, "A *secret* place."

Zeus pressed his face against the helmet for a closer look, but his ragged breath fogged up the surface. Wiping it off with a paw, he spied the sandy bottom, a few swaying plants, the rocky base of Santorini extending in both directions, and—"Whoa, is that a fang?" He pointed at a triangular object jutting up from the floor nearby. It was larger than his head, gleaming white, its sharp edges serrated.

"Not a fang," Poseidon replied. "A tooth."

"Fang. Tooth. Same difference." Zeus hunched down to inspect the arrowhead-shaped object.

"What creature did that fang, er, tooth belong to?" Demeter asked.

"Shark," Poseidon answered. "Great white."

"Any of these great sharks live around here?" Zeus's voice quivered slightly as he glanced around.

"I wish," Poseidon said. "I'd order them to kick Proteus out of my realm."

Zeus let out a sigh of relief.

"A fish that big could swallow Proteus whole," Demeter remarked.

"It could certainly swallow us whole, helmet and all," Zeus added.

"I'm counting on that." Poseidon pointed his trident along the side of Santorini. Zeus noticed some smooth white stones inlaid at the base of the seamount just a few feet away. The seahorses hauled the dive helmet in front of the white stones, and Zeus did a double take. What he'd taken for smooth rocks were actually jaws,

absolutely massive, filled with arrowhead-shaped teeth.
They were snapped shut, but one missing tooth at the
bottom made a small gap. The jaws were easily large
enough to swallow the dive helmet.

Before Zeus and Demeter could ask any questions,
Poseidon jabbed his trident into a small hole in the hinge
of the jaws. With a rush of bubbles, they sprang open,
revealing a hidden portal to a narrow canyon that ran
through the seamount.

"The good ol' Santorini Shortcut!" Poseidon
exclaimed. "Told you this was a special place. Let's go
find your boat."

CHAPTER 17

THE SEAHORSES BOLTED THROUGH THE jaws, yanking the dive helmet behind them, slipping between the serrated teeth—rows of them—with plenty of room on either side. The helmet's air hose slid though the groove left by the missing tooth, threading through the white razors of the jaw. Poseidon brought up the rear as the group rushed into the canyon. Between Zeus's feet, the rolling see-through floor of the helmet revealed that the canyon had no bottom. They were racing above an abyss. He detected the faintest trace of a red glow far below—it was molten lava that followed the course of the canyon.

The shark-jaw entrance dwindled behind them

and soon faded from view. They rolled along the canyon's narrow rock walls for what felt like an eternity. Zeus's stomach churned each time he peeked down at the abyss, so he stared ahead, hoping for an end to this claustrophobic portion of their Oddest Sea voyage.

Suddenly, the canyon's exit loomed. Zeus and Demeter blinked at the explosion of color as they emerged on the other side of the seamount into a coral garden. Tubes, spires, fans, and antler-like structures towered atop rocks around them, practically glowing in every rainbow color from red to violet. The day was dawning on the surface realm above.

"We better find the *Argo ½* quick," Zeus said.

Just as he said it, Arion brought the team to a halt and whinnied. Poseidon followed his minion's gaze. He found a red hull, completely cracked down the middle. A deep green coral spiral rose between the two broken halves. The bow of the vessel rested atop a raggedy Zeus Deuce.

"Found it!" Demeter exclaimed.

"You came in that thing?" Poseidon puffed up in surprise.

"She's a seaworthy vessel," Zeus said defensively about the wreckage.

"Doesn't seem so seaworthy now, Zeus." Demeter surveyed the wreckage.

"Awww, this is an easy fix!" Zeus scoffed. "Hey, Poseidon, do you have some chewing gum—"

A haunting melody, just at the limits of hearing, silenced Zeus. It was a wild, soaring harmony of at least two voices. Suddenly Zeus wanted to focus on nothing else. The tune was all he wanted. It was comforting, warm, familiar, catchy. His spirits soared when the tune got louder. Beside him, Demeter was just as transfixed.

But they were ripped from their stupor by a sudden commotion. Poseidon had puffed up nearby and was trying to pull his crown over his ears.

"Oh no! It's that ghastly song again. I'm not going to fall under its spell this time!" Poseidon's tail fins blurred as he started to speed away. The seahorses took off after him but stopped short when the dive helmet slipped from its rigging. Poseidon's minions carefully reset the helmet in its harness. They had also begun to growl. The noise was deep, like a low hum. The seahorses appeared to be vibrating with it. Despite the drowsiness washing over him, Zeus couldn't help but notice them.

He shook the cobwebs from his head. "Hey! What about us?!" Zeus called after Poseidon.

"Never fear! I'll return with help!" Poseidon's voice faded as he zoomed back into the canyon.

Zeus and Demeter couldn't protest because the melody had grown even louder, its source closer. They slumped in the dive helmet as the humming seahorses hovered helplessly nearby, too late to pull the Olympians to safety. Zeus and Demeter had fallen under the Sirens' spell.

CHAPTER 18

ZEUS INHABITED A COZY WORLD BETWEEN wakefulness and dreamland—a world he never wanted to leave. Dimly, he noticed two creatures swim into view. They were sleek and graceful, with dark tresses that flowed behind them. Their scaly bodies reflected the rainbow colors of the coral around them. They left a shimmering froth in their wake, almost as though they were aquatic shooting stars.

Each Siren sang in a different key and tone, as if they were musical instruments in a micro-symphony. It became hard to tell which one was singing which part, but that was unimportant. What mattered was the melody itself, haunting and hypnotic.

The creatures circled the dive helmet twice, then

settled above the sunken wreckage of the *Argo ½*.
But their compelling tune abruptly stopped. Zeus
and Demeter both snapped out of their stupor with a
feeling of intense disappointment just as a third Siren—
this one larger—swam up to join the others.

"What ... what happened to the song?" Demeter
shook her head.

Zeus rubbed his eyes and took in the musical
creatures from his dreamland. Now that the spell was
broken, he saw their true form: slimy, spotted eel-like
things. Each had a pair of stubby arms and stalks of
external gills that dangled behind their bulbous heads.
Zeus couldn't believe he had confused those stringy gills
for fine hair. He noted that the water still shimmered in
their wake. His disappointment became relief that he
was no longer under their spell.

But before he could say a word, one of the Sirens
spoke directly to Zeus in an excited, wavering tone.
"Oh, Proteus, my lord, forgive us!"

The second creature darted in front of the first.
"We Sirens had no idea you had morphed into the king
of the gods!"

"And we exalt that you have bested that arrogant rodent!" The first Siren pointed with one fat arm at Zeus Deuce pinned beneath the wreckage.

The third Siren—the large newcomer—unleashed a deep, raspy laugh.

Zeus looked from Zeus Deuce to the creatures, utterly confused. He was about to correct the Sirens when Demeter leapt in front of him. She raised four legs in a gesture of surrender.

"Yes, yes," Demeter wailed. "Cunning Proteus here"—she nodded toward Zeus—"has defeated my brave king."

Zeus's brow furrowed while Demeter carried on. Finally he broke into a broad grin as he grasped the situation. He puffed out his chest and put his paws on his hips. "Ha-hah!" he laughed loudly, trying to match what he remembered of Proteus's oddly deep voice. "Yes, it was a close battle of wits and, uh, more wits." He struggled for what to say next. The Sirens watched him in silence. "Zeus is just so sharp and powerful!" Zeus said, still imitating Proteus. "He nearly won!"

Demeter cringed. The Sirens said nothing.

"But ... uh ... I managed to give the king of the gods a poetic defeat," Zeus quickly added. "I buried him beneath his own boat!" He lifted his chin in a show of arrogance while the Sirens circled Zeus Deuce in a tizzy of appreciation. "And, of course, I managed to capture his minion in the process." He jabbed a thumb at Demeter.

"Clearly we Olympians are no match for you, cunning sea lord," Demeter cried. She dropped to the bottom of the helmet and pretended to weep. "Oh, our foolish, foolish king."

"Um, right," Zeus agreed halfheartedly.

"Our loudmouth, egotistical king," Demeter wailed.

"Okay, that's enough out of you," Zeus said sharply.

The largest Siren stopped circling. "But if you're here, Proteus, then who did we leave lounging on Poseidon's throne?" This Siren's voice was the deepest of the group.

The other two creatures pulled to a sudden halt, their gill stalks quivering, as they peered fearfully in the direction they had come from.

Zeus's mind raced. "Don't tell me you fools let

Poseidon retake my throne?!" he roared. The Sirens quivered.

Two of them raced off through the corals, leaving their trails of incandescent froth. The largest Siren lingered, a strange smirk on his bulbous face. "Fear not, my lord. Follow in our wake, and we'll have Poseidon in our thrall by the time you arrive." He darted after the other two Sirens.

Zeus rapped on the dive helmet. "Arion! After those creatures!" But the black seahorse only whinnied.

"Shouldn't we wait for Poseidon to return?" Demeter asked. "Maybe the other Olympians can help?"

"Help with what?" Zeus raised his arms in exasperation. "You heard that Siren—they think they're on their way to put Poseidon to sleep with their magical song. But they'll really be sending Proteus to Snoozeville! We can go right now and capture him!" He turned to Arion. "I said giddyup!"

This time, the seahorses spurred into action, following the Sirens' glowing wake at full gallop, even faster than before. The helmet shimmied in its harness.

"We'll wrap up this whole Oddest Sea journey and be

home before breakfast!" Zeus reassured Demeter. They were both sprinting to keep up with the rapidly spinning helmet.

"When do things ever work out that way?" Demeter mumbled. But she kept her head down and decided to concentrate on her footing as they raced toward Poseidon's throne.

CHAPTER 19

THE HELMET ROLLED THROUGH A CANOPY of coral fans and onto a sprawling stretch of seafloor. The seahorse team strained to follow the sleek Sirens, which had raced far ahead. Fortunately, their shimmering trail lingered, helping the seahorses track them.

Demeter had resigned herself to bouncing and rolling along inside the helmet. "Just tell me when we get there," she said to Zeus, as she curled up into a protective bug ball. A wilted bit of lettuce from her sash had broken off and lodged on her antennae.

"I ... I don't think I can do this for much longer," Zeus replied, nearly out of breath.

They barreled through a seaweed forest and emerged

in an open area with a broad pathway paved with smooth, multicolored stones. The Sirens' glowing wake still lingered in the water. A statue of a bearded, muscle-bound human stood next to the glittering path, as if guarding it. The figure wore a chiton and crown and wielded a trident nearly as long as Poseidon's. A plate across the bottom of the statue bore a single word in a strange, unreadable script.

Suddenly, a shower of bubbles exploded from the figure's crown as its arm lowered the trident, blocking their path.

"Whooaaaa," Zeus ordered the seahorses. The dive helmet halted just before the lowered trident.

Demeter unrolled from her ball. "Are we there?"

"Who's that guy supposed to be?" Zeus asked, paws on his knees, panting. He glared at the statue barring their way.

"I dunno." Demeter shrugged. "Just some human? They all look alike." She was more interested in the glittering wake that was quickly fading. "Where are the Sirens?"

"They swam right past the statue, and down this fancy path."

"Good that we stopped here, actually," Demeter said. "This seems like it could be the entrance to Poseidon's throne area."

"Right," Zeus agreed. "Right! We'll let the Sirens work their sleepy song on Proteus, then sneak in for the capture!"

Demeter waved at the trident. "So do we just go around this, or ..."

Another shower of bubbles burst from the figure's head. The trident lifted, opening the path to Poseidon's throne.

"I'll take this as a sign," Zeus said. "Arion, giddyup!"

The seahorses zoomed ahead, sending Demeter tumbling backward again. Zeus leapt right into a sprint. The thought of capturing Proteus had given him a second wind.

CHAPTER 20

ZEUS COULDN'T HELP BUT WHISTLE AT THE elaborate decor as they drew closer to Poseidon's marine sanctum. They passed a stone replica of a fine Greek galley, its oars pumped by an invisible crew, each stroke releasing a stream of bubbles. Coral overhangs brushed over their heads. Ruins of temples and other crumbling structures littered the sandy bottom. "How come we don't have cool stuff like this on Mount Olympus?" asked Demeter.

"It's not that cool," Zeus huffed, even though he was busy admiring a trio of gleaming pyramids that could have come from ancient Egypt, an era even before the Greeks. "All this stuff seems tacky to me."

They passed through an outer courtyard of soft coral

and elaborate statuary of 11 human men and women, arranged in a half-circle, all wearing chitons and wielding accessories: spears, bows, harps. Each was animated like the trident-wielding statue at the path's entrance. The largest figure, standing at the center of the half-circle, hefted a thunderbolt over his head. "If I didn't know any better," Zeus said, studying the biggest figure, "I'd say these were statues of humans pretending to be us!"

Demeter giggled. "That's absurd."

They crossed onto a round dais formed from smooth black stone, possibly onyx. Both Olympians lurched face-first into the wall of the helmet as the seahorse team brought it to an abrupt halt. Zeus was about to protest when he saw they had reached the throne at the center of the dais. The throne was formed from an indentation in a titanic, brain-shaped orange coral covered with sharp ridges and overhung with vibrant sea plants that swayed in the current. But the seat was empty. The three Sirens swam in a slow circle around it, creating a halo of glittering water in their wake.

Zeus addressed the creatures. "Where's Prot—I mean

Poseidon?" he asked in his faux-deep Proteus impersonation.

"He's asleep, my lord," answered the largest Siren. "Just as you ordered."

Zeus spun around. He saw coral fans and the statuary of the courtyard, but no sign of a sleeping shape-changer. "Asleep where?"

"We wanted to present him to you properly," the biggest Siren continued. "Come, Proteus," he beckoned Zeus to the empty throne, "resume your true octopus form and take your seat as the new sea lord."

Zeus glanced at the throne uneasily. The silence stretched on. Bubbles burbled from the statues nearby. The seahorses shifted restlessly. The Sirens waited expectantly. Demeter cleared her throat and nudged Zeus. "They're getting suspicious," she hissed. "Say something."

Zeus hesitated. Then, in his fake Proteus voice, he said, "I appreciate the thought, minions, but I've grown quite accustomed to this furry form." He slapped his belly. "And besides, I need to watch over this nuisance." He gestured at Demeter. "Plenty of time to kick back in the ol' power chair later."

The largest Siren swam within inches of the dive helmet. "Oh, take your seat now, king. We insist. Sirens!" On command, the two smaller Sirens bolted toward the helmet and grabbed its air hose with their stubby arms. Before the seahorses could react, the Sirens had yanked the helmet free from its harness.

Arion and the other seahorses growled their low, humming growl in anger, but they were still tethered to the helmet rigging and were unable to help as the Sirens dragged Zeus and Demeter roughly to the throne. Arion managed to shake off his harness, but he was too late: The Sirens had already lashed the helmet to Poseidon's throne by wrapping the air hose around it. Zeus and Demeter were trapped at the bottom of the Aegean.

Arion dashed to the throne to undo the lashing. "Atta boy!" Zeus rooted him on. "Save us!"

But before Arion could unwrap the air hose, he was thwacked across the snout and sent flying by the largest Siren. The other seahorses, still hung up in the helmet rigging, swam clumsily to their leader's aid. The Sirens swarmed them.

The large Siren remained at the dais, a smug expression on his face as he watched his companions pursue the harried seahorse team into the dim distance. When they were gone, he turned to the helmet. "No rescue for you this time, Zeus the Mighty." He uttered a deep, raspy laugh that sounded frighteningly familiar to Demeter.

"Uh, Zeus ...?" she whispered.

Zeus was too distracted by his own fury. "I liked you Sirens a lot more when you just sang catchy tunes!" he yelled.

"I don't think this one's a Siren," Demeter said quietly.

The Siren grinned at them as his body began stretching and shrinking, as though it couldn't decide what shape it should be. A black inky cloud expanded around the Siren, obscuring his pulsating body. Finally, from the cloud emerged a speckled octopus with beady eyes on a fat head. Eight striped tentacles sprouted from its body and swayed in the current like overcooked spaghetti noodles.

"Proteus, I presume?" Demeter asked flatly, trying

to sound unimpressed.

Zeus's face wrinkled in disgust at the sight of Proteus's true form. "You can change into anything you want, and you choose to look like *that*?"

The octopus's laugh boomed inside the helmet. "This has been a productive day," he rasped. "I had merely planned to conquer the water realm. Now I've ensnared Zeus, king of the land—and so easily, as well!" He laughed again.

Zeus smirked and waved toward the dais. "The way I see it, I'm the one sitting on the throne."

Proteus stopped laughing and spun in place, releasing another cloud of ink. His tentacles whipped at the helmet, driving it into the sharp coral ridges of Poseidon's throne. *CRACK!* A hairline fracture formed on the surface of the helmet. A drop of inky seawater leaked through the crack.

Demeter reached up to wipe away the water. Another drop followed, then another, until a slow but steady stream dripped through the crack and began to pool on the bottom of the helmet. "This really isn't what we needed right now," she muttered as she mopped up the puddle with the wet rag.

Proteus, pleased with his effort, returned Zeus's smirk. "The way I see it," he said, mimicking Zeus, "your time on the throne is quite limited."

CHAPTER 21

THE ARGO HAD BEEN ON THE WATER FOR AT least an hour, and it was making good speed with Ares and Hermes at each oar. The vessel easily navigated the ocean swells, which had died down considerably. Athena turned from her position in the stern holding the tiller to observe her vessel's wake. Land was just a hazy line on the horizon. She turned back and saw that the vessel had begun to drift to the right. Hermes had stopped paddling and was nursing one of her wings.

"Hermes, focus!" Athena shouted. "You're throwing us off course!"

Hermes sheepishly called back to Athena. "My wings ain't used to this heavy liftin'. I'm a ground-bound bird."

"Don't worry, buddy!" Ares exclaimed happily. "I got enough muscle for the both of us." The war god shifted to straddle the deck of the *Argo*, which tilted alarmingly for a moment before righting itself. He grabbed an oar in each forepaw and started pumping them with gusto. The *Argo* resumed its course.

"Where are we going, anyway?" Hermes asked as she stepped out of Ares's way.

"That way." Athena nodded forward.

"Okay." Hermes craned her neck to see over the bow. "For how long?"

"Until we see something—some sign of Poseidon, Zeus, or Demeter."

"Okay," Hermes repeated.

"Ahoy!" said a familiar, confident voice from just ahead. "I said, 'Ahoy!'"

"Who's that? Do we have an Olympian overboard?" Hermes cried, checking to make sure Ares and Athena were still aboard.

"It's Poseidon!" Ares exclaimed. He spun excitedly in a circle, nearly swamping the vessel, before returning to the middle of the deck.

Athena leaned over the side. "Poseidon! Are we ever glad to see you!"

The pufferfish bobbed in the water and admired the *Argo*. "It's a wonder you got that thing to float," he said. "Wait, where's your figurehead?"

"The figurehead!" Hermes clapped a wing against her rubbery beard. "I knew we forgot something!"

"Too late for that now!" Athena said. "Have you seen Zeus and Demeter?"

"Indeed I have!" Poseidon said excitedly. "They've

fallen under the spell of the Sirens!"

"Sirens?" Athena repeated. "That explains the hypnotizing song when we launched."

"They're the minions of Proteus," Poseidon continued. "The shape-changer who duped me!"

"Duped you how?" Ares asked.

"I'll tell you later." Poseidon spun away from them in the water. "Zeus and Demeter need our help. Follow me!" The sea lord dashed off to the east, leaving an easy-to-follow wake.

The Olympians watched him in stunned silence for a moment. "Follow that fish!" Athena commanded, back at the tiller. Ares began pumping the oars with renewed strength. The *Argo* jolted into motion.

Hermes shielded her eyes with one of her wings to track Poseidon's progress. "You know it's bad luck to sail without a figurehead, right?"

Athena didn't answer. She was focused on the horizon and following Poseidon.

CHAPTER 22

ZEUS STOOD AT THE CRACK IN THE HELMET, trying to plug it with a paw. Water steadily seeped around his furry fingers. "This isn't doing anything." He pulled his paw away in frustration and examined it. "It's just making me pruny."

Demeter's rag was so wet that it couldn't absorb any more water. The puddle on the floor was growing. "We have to do something."

"You can drown—eventually," Proteus rasped. The octopus hovered just above the helmet, which remained firmly lashed by its air hose to Poseidon's coral throne.

"Don't you have better things to do than just float there and gloat?" Demeter snapped.

"Ooh, I know," Zeus offered. "Maybe morph into an

anchor and toss yourself into an abyss?"

"Or maybe go find your weird musical minions or something?" Demeter suggested.

Proteus chuckled. "I'm sure you would just love it if I wandered off so that pufferfish or his seahorses could swoop to your rescue." Proteus's beady eyes narrowed. "I'm actually hoping they do show up. I have plans for them." He laughed again.

"What do you keep laughing at?" Zeus asked. "Nothing you just said was a joke." He scratched his chin. "Do you even know how humor works?"

Demeter had dropped the rag and stood up. "You said you're *hoping* they show up? Can't you foresee the future? Shouldn't you know?"

"Bah," Zeus waved dismissively at Proteus. "These fortune-telling types never know anything about the future."

Proteus scowled. "My powers of foresight are unparalleled."

"Uh-huh, yeah, so are mine." Zeus closed his eyes and held a paw to his forehead. "I predict that your predictions are just gobbledygook!" But when the expanding seawater puddle reached his toes, his eyes shot open in alarm, and he scooched sideways out of it.

"I do not need super abilities to see you're not long for this world." Proteus snorted a brief laugh at the helmet's rising waterline.

Zeus clapped his paws. "Aha! So you admit you don't have super powers! I told you these fortune-teller types were frauds, Demeter!"

Proteus sighed. "I've nothing to prove to you. Even if I wanted to reveal your future to you, you haven't met a crucial requirement."

"Yeah, yeah, we haven't lulled you to sleep and captured you," Demeter replied in a bored voice. "The Oracle told us."

"You have not," Proteus agreed. "But there's no harm in me having a peek for my own amusement." His face suddenly went slack, and his skin began to pulsate. He started releasing flurries of ink. "I'm sure I need only the briefest glimpse into your future to see how this will end ..." Proteus froze, his voice fading.

Zeus and Demeter watched the octopus expectantly. But Proteus remained still. When he listed sideways and began to sink, Zeus waved his paws in his face.

"Heyo, eight-legs? Anybody home in there?"

Suddenly, Proteus began to jerk. His upper body was morphing rapid-fire through a series of shapes, not all of them animals. He transformed so quickly that Zeus and Demeter couldn't register what they were seeing. There might have been a ship, then a large, four-legged animal.

"Was that ... was that a horse?" Demeter asked, trying to keep up.

"I think Proteus is broken," Zeus replied.

Just as quickly as the shape-changing spree had started, it stopped. The inky water cleared. Proteus returned to his normal size and octopus shape, exhaling a geyser of bubbles. He was visibly exhausted. "Oh my," he finally muttered. "I've peeked into some bleak futures before, but nothing as bleak as *that!*"

"Bleak as what?" Zeus asked, confused.

Proteus still seemed dazed, but he responded. "War." The word hung in the silence.

"War?" Demeter squeaked. "War with who?"

Proteus shook his head. "I've already told you more than you deserve to hear."

"You say you see a war in our future?" Zeus double-checked, sounding almost relieved.

Proteus nodded.

"And you promise that your powers of foresight are unparalleled?"

The octopus nodded again.

Demeter whispered, "Why do you sound like this war stuff is a good thing?"

"It means we're not going to drown in here!" Zeus splashed the rising water for effect. "I'll take it!"

"Enough!" Proteus rasped. "The future is fluid—as you're about to find out!"

Proteus pulsated and shape-shifted his tentacles into a conch shell the size of his head. He blew into the shell, releasing a spray of bubbles.

Zeus didn't hear the shell's noise so much as feel it.

SPOOOSH! A wave of pressure bowled across him and Demeter, knocking the helmet into the throne. The crack widened, and the water now streamed in much faster.

"What was that?! Proteus, what did you do?" Demeter demanded.

"I summoned an old friend," the octopus answered as the conch shell morphed back into tentacles. "I believe you've met before."

"Scylla." Demeter scanned the churning, murky depths around them.

Zeus shook himself off. "The future is fluid," Zeus repeated Proteus's words. "As in water. Oh, I get it now."

Proteus laughed his deep, raspy laugh.

"Still not actually a joke, though," Zeus groused as Proteus jetted away into the waves.

CHAPTER 23

ARES HAD BEEN ROWING THE ARGO'S OARS
furiously to keep up with Poseidon's wake.
Suddenly, the pufferfish broke the surface
and waved his trident. "Hold fast!" he yelled.

"Ease off, Ares!" Athena commanded from the tiller.
The *Argo* drifted to a halt. "What's up, Poseidon?"
Athena asked. "Have you found them?"

"Did you hear that?" Poseidon asked, ignoring her
question.

Ares cocked his head. "Hear what?"

"It was a blast across the entire sea." Poseidon
pressed his face into the water and squinted, listening.
He came back up. "It was almost like ... like an alarm,
or a summons."

Hermes tilted her head, her crest of feathers wobbling. "A summons for what?"

Poseidon turned to answer, and his wide eyes went even wider. "For that!" he exclaimed.

The *Argo* lurched left, then right, then rose straight up by several inches as the Olympians on board scrambled to keep their balance.

A sucker-covered trunk was sliding along the bottom of the *Argo*'s hull. The dark shape seemed endless, like a slimy rope.

The massive tentacle finally sank below the waves. The *Argo* resettled on the water's surface; its crew watched in stunned silence as the creature's endless body slid beneath them. It was going in the direction Poseidon had been leading them.

"Don't just stand there!" Poseidon waved his trident at the tentacle. "Follow it!"

"Follow it?!" Hermes squawked.

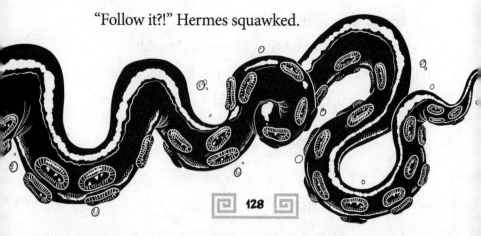

"I don't even know what *it* is," Athena added.

"It's Scylla!" Poseidon yelled. "Proteus's pet sea monster. It's no doubt on its way to finish Zeus and Demeter! We must head it off!"

"Ooh, I'll take its head off!" Ares exclaimed. Before anyone could respond, the pug leapt right off the deck, curling up his meatloaf-shaped body and hitting the water with a splash that soaked Athena and Hermes.

The pug landed on Scylla and sank his powerful jaws into the creature's black hide. Streams of bubbles erupted where Ares's teeth had punctured Scylla's body. The sea monster writhed and picked up its pace, but Ares held firm. He was along for the ride.

The pufferfish sighed.

"Well, ya did tell him to head it off," Hermes said to Poseidon as he zoomed away in pursuit. Hermes shook out her soggy wings, rattling her silver chain, and took up both the *Argo*'s oars. They were underway again, although much more slowly without Ares's muscle.

Athena leapt to the tiller and yanked hard to adjust their course. They couldn't let Poseidon and the sea monster leave them behind.

CHAPTER 24

ZEUS AND DEMETER WERE STARING UP AT the worrying crack in the dive helmet when a dark, slimy tentacle, thick as a tree trunk, stretched toward them from above.

"So that's what Scylla looks like from below," Zeus said. "A giant, monster ... noodle." The creature's tentacle seemed to extend infinitely into the gloom.

In moments, Scylla had wrapped its sucker-covered arm around the helmet and the throne once, twice. In just three loops, it engulfed the helmet. Zeus noted that the creature didn't really have a face—no mouth, no nose, no eyes. It was all tentacle, teeth-rimmed suckers, and slime, right up to its tip, which was like the head of a fat black worm. The creature convulsed, squeezing.

It was trying to crush the helmet.

The walls started to flex around Zeus and Demeter.

"How much more pressure can this thing take, Zeus?" Demeter asked.

"Oh, plenty," Zeus said. He confidently slapped the wall. *CRACK!*

The fracture had expanded again. Water now ran in rivulets to Zeus's paw.

Scylla squeezed again. *CRICK! CRACK!* Two new small cracks formed.

Despite the rising flood, Zeus stood tall and puffed out his chiton. "Get ready, Demeter—we're about to go for a swim."

Demeter sucked in a deep breath.

But Scylla's attack suddenly stopped as the monster released the helmet and retracted its body. Demeter exhaled in relief as she watched the titanic tentacle move back up toward the surface. On its way, Scylla swatted at a meatloaf-shaped form clamped to the upper reaches of its body.

"Is that ... is that who I think it is?" Zeus asked.

CHAPTER 25

"**A**RES!" DEMETER EXCLAIMED.

There was no mistaking the war god's wrinkled mug and Spartan war helmet, which somehow had stayed on his head as Scylla dragged him to the depths. The monster corkscrewed its noodle-like trunk to shake him off, but Ares held firm, bubbles streaming from his jaws which were sunk deep into the beast's hide.

"I think he thinks he's rescuing *us* from Scylla!" Zeus's mouth hung open.

Scylla's body shot downward and raced past Zeus and Demeter, dragging the hitchhiking war god within inches of their vantage point. They could hear him howling with bubbly delight. Ares's expression was

unmistakable—even with a mouthful of sea monster. He was smiling.

"I think Ares *is* rescuing us from Scylla," Demeter responded.

"Look at that Scylla-eating grin," said a familiar, muffled voice beside them.

Zeus and Demeter jumped when they saw Poseidon hovering above his throne, watching the battle unfold above them. "Ares is really in his element—a natural sea dog!"

"Poseidon!" Demeter shouted.

"Poseidon, my fuzzy butt." Zeus crossed his arms and turned his back. "Nice try, Proteus!"

Poseidon opened his mouth to respond—then ducked to escape Scylla and Ares charging over his head. Ares dug his hind legs into Scylla's hide; the monster suddenly bent and shot off in a new direction.

"I'd swear Ares is getting the upper hand on that beast!" Poseidon said.

"Well, you're not getting the upper hand on us this time, *Proteus*!" Zeus snapped.

"Why must you always doubt my identity?" Poseidon

broke his gaze from the drama above and peered around. "Where is that impostor, anyway?"

"Proteus was just here," Demeter explained.

"But now he's gone and you're here," Zeus added. "So you can understand why we're a little skeptical that you are who you say you are."

"Fascinating." Poseidon, ignoring Zeus, pointed his trident at Ares. "He's actually getting air from the creature's hide. He's breathing underwater!"

"Quit trying to change the subject, *Proteus!*" Zeus banged on the inside of the helmet next to Poseidon's head. "We're not falling for your phony-baloney act ever again!"

Poseidon was about to respond, but then did a double take when he noticed Zeus was standing waist deep in water. Demeter was standing on the tips of her legs. "Oh dear," he said. "You two air-breathing gods are about to need some air yourselves." He used his trident to unwrap the air hose securing the helmet to his throne.

"QUIT CHANGING THE SUBJE—"

SCHWOOP! The untethered helmet shot toward the surface of the Aegean. Bits of lettuce, the soaked rag, and other debris bobbed around Zeus and Demeter in the

flood as they rocketed upward.

"Athena and Hermes will help you!" Poseidon shouted up at them. "Ares and I will take care of this monster." He swam fast after Scylla.

CHAPTER 26

N THE SURFACE, HERMES WAS WAVING her wings to keep her balance on the *Argo*'s deck, and Athena dug her claws into the tiller to keep from getting pitched into the suddenly swirling seas. Waves battered the hull of the vessel, sending it spinning and pitching.

"Why'd the sea get all loosey-goosey?" Hermes asked. "That Scylla beast still skulkin' below us?"

Athena, peering over the side of the deck, was about to answer when ... *BLOOP!* A massive bubble broke the waterline just ahead of the *Argo*'s bow.

"Yep, Scylla's skulkin' all right," a familiar voice called out.

"Zeus?!" Athena and Hermes exclaimed. They were

staring down at Poseidon's dive helmet, which hovered in place despite the churning sea.

"In the flesh!" Zeus buffed the thunderbolt emblem on his chest. His voice was surprisingly loud despite him being inside the airtight helmet. He appeared safe, clean, and dry.

"Where'd you come from?" Athena asked.

"And how'd you end up in Poseidon's helmet?" added Hermes.

"And where's Demeter?" Athena added as she cast around her gaze for the goddess of the harvest.

Zeus raised his hands. "All your questions are really good and super important," he said warmly, although his eyes looked strangely distant. "Thank you soooo much for your concern."

Hermes and Athena exchanged uneasy glances.

"But right now, I really need your help!" He pressed his paws together in a pleading gesture. "Actually, Ares, Poseidon, and Demeter need your help! They're down there battling Proteus and his superscary pet, Scylla."

"Down *there*?" Hermes had joined Athena in peering over the deck.

"Yes!" Zeus replied enthusiastically. "And they're in way over their heads, as you can imagine."

Athena squinted into the water. "Okay, okay," she said. "What can we do to help?"

"We'll need the whole team to beat Proteus—he's just too cunning!" Zeus sounded like he almost admired the shape-changer.

"Right, mojo to the rescue," Hermes added.

Zeus's head tilted slightly, a tic the other Olympians had never seen before. He stared at Athena and Hermes with his odd eyes before saying, "Nah, we don't need Mojo. The three of us can handle Scylla ourselves." Then his expression brightened, and he resumed his cheerfully urgent demeanor. "Now everyone into the water! I order you, as your king!"

Athena and Hermes didn't move. "I don't know, king." Athena dipped a single claw over the side and casually tested the water. "This sort of battle is right in Mojo's wheelhouse." She paused for Zeus's reaction.

The hamster blinked at her from inside the helmet.

"And ya know how Mojo gets if we don't invite her on these missions," Hermes added, catching on.

Zeus stood frozen in awkward silence. He seemed about to speak when *WHOOOOSH!* Another dive helmet broke the surface and splashed down alongside the *Argo*. This one was two-thirds full of cloudy water. Bits of wilted lettuce were plastered on its inner walls. A dirty rag swirled around Zeus and Demeter, who were treading water.

When the Zeus inside this helmet registered the other helmet—and the other Zeus standing in it—he yelled, "That's not me!" He slapped a pruny paw against the helmet's grimy wall. His voice sounded muffled, but

his words were clear. "That's Proteus!"

"Yeah, we kinda figured that out," Hermes said matter-of-factly. "Good to see you two safe and sound!"

"We'll be a lot safer once we get out of this leaky tub." Demeter pushed at the helmet's faceplate above her, but it wouldn't budge. "Someone mind popping the top?"

"Happy to!" Hermes reached down and tried to work the faceplate hatch open.

"So what do we do with Zeus Deuce over there?" Athena jabbed her paw at Proteus, who was watching them angrily from his pristine helmet. He was still disguised as Zeus.

"Oh please." Zeus sneered at Proteus. "That imposter's got nothin' on *my* Zeus Deuce."

Proteus's expression brightened when a familiar sound reached them: angelic singing, two voices in harmony. It was a haunting tune.

"It's the Sirens!" Zeus exclaimed, ducking under the water in his helmet to try to block the sound. But the song was even louder there. He returned to the surface, already nearly dazed. "They'll send us to nappy time if we're not careful!"

"I have a more ... permanent plan for you than 'nappy time,' Zeus," Proteus said in a raspy voice. The Sirens' voices dropped to an ominous tone as the dive helmet surrounding him dissolved into a cloud of black ink. The dark cloud obscured Proteus, but when he emerged his eight striped tentacles and bulbous body were visible. He had assumed his default form.

Hermes was ignoring Proteus's shape-shifting spectacle. She had finally worked her wingtips into the latch that would open Zeus and Demeter's escape hatch. But before she could spring the release, Proteus wrapped his tentacles around the helmet's lifeline and disappeared in a swoosh of inky water with the flooded helmet in tow.

The Sirens resumed their hypnotic singing with full-throated gusto.

"He took 'em!" Hermes turned to Athena. "He took Zeus and Demeter!"

Athena didn't respond. She wore a dreamy expression as the Sirens' hypnotic melody swelled in her ears.

CHAPTER 27

THE GOD OF WAR WAS HAVING THE TIME OF his life.

Scylla was raging in the deep, gyrating in violent corkscrews and stomach-churning loops, even skidding along sharp corals and the sandy seafloor—all in an attempt to shake off the pugnacious pug attached to its hide.

"Wooooooo-hooooooo!" Ares whooped a stream of bubbles around the hunk of slimy Scylla skin locked between his jaws. This wild ride reminded Ares of a game he often played with Artie. She'd hold a rope that ended in a knot—Artie called it the Gordian knot—and Ares would clamp his jaws onto it while Artie towed him hither and yon, trying to shake him free. Ares didn't know who Gordian was, but whoever it was, they could tie a heck of a knot.

Scylla dove hard toward the courtyard, turning its body so Ares would plow through the half-circle of animated statues. It was a perfect strike; the statues bounced off Ares's Spartan war helmet and went flying in every direction in a shower of bubbles. One statue's accessory wedged in Ares's teeth. He almost lost his grip on Scylla, until he used his tongue to dislodge the sharp piece from his gums. "Haaahaahee!" the war god giggled, enraging Scylla further.

"We're here to stop the beast, Ares!" Poseidon called after him. The sea lord had been watching from the courtyard. "This isn't playtime!"

"I know!" Ares replied as Scylla whipped him through a loop. "Playtime is never this fun!"

Poseidon shook his head. "Ares's jaws just aren't up to the job," he muttered. "Jaws ..." he repeated. "Jaws!" He waved his trident to get the pug's attention. "Ares! We need bigger jaws!" But Scylla had completed a hairpin turn and was now zooming toward the courtyard. Poseidon carefully aimed the trident,

pointing the tines at the oncoming beast. "HNGH!" He heaved with all his might. The trident flew true, piercing the monster's sucker-covered face and unleashing an explosion of bubbles where the fork-shaped weapon sank deeply into its flesh. The creature recoiled, writhing in pain and outrage.

"Like that nifty nose-piercing?!" Poseidon taunted Scylla. "Come and get me!" He spun and dashed down the glittering path, away from the dais.

Scylla sprang into motion, skimming the seafloor in pursuit of the pufferfish. Ares maintained the iron grip with his jaws, whooping in excitement as fans of coral and seaweed whipped against his face.

CHAPTER 28

BACK ON THE ARGO, HERMES WATCHED THE
Sirens swirl around them, creating a circle of
glowing froth and filling the air with their
irritating tune. At least Hermes thought it was irritating.
Athena seemed asleep on her feet, gazing dreamily
into the sea while the *Argo* drifted aimlessly on the
ocean swells.

"Now I know how that Odysseus guy felt," Hermes
groused, then smacked a wing against her forehead.
"The feathers!" she yelled at Athena. "Remember the
feathers!"

Athena blinked. "Wha?" Her head swiveled
sluggishly in Hermes's direction.

"The feathers!" Hermes plucked at the feathers

tucked in Athena's collar, making the owl charm tinkle. She held them in front of Athena's face. Athena didn't react.

"Fine, I'll do it!" Hermes crammed the feathers into each of Athena's fuzzy ears.

The cat's blue eyes began to refocus. "Wha-what's this?" She reached a paw up to her ears and began rubbing at the feathers.

Hermes held up her wings to stop her. "KEEP 'EM IN!" she yelled. "They block the Sirens' snooze song!"

Athena nodded and noticed the Sirens circling the *Argo*. "RIGHT, LIKE THE WAX FROM THE ORACLE'S LESSON."

Hermes winced. "YOU DON'T HAVE TO YELL!" she yelled. "I CAN HEAR YA JUST FINE."

Athena gave a sheepish look and whispered to Hermes, "Right. Sorry."

Hermes put her wings on her hips and glared at the Sirens. "Y'all thought you could put my friend to sleep? You know I'm the goddess of sleep, right?" The Sirens' gill stalks quivered in fury. Their song took on a desperate tone before it cut off abruptly.

Athena, back to her alert self, scanned the horizon and spotted a disturbance in the distant waves. A torrent of bubbles percolated to the surface, followed by a geyser of water. "Hermes, to the oars!" she commanded. "Those bubbles might just lead us to our fellow Olympians!"

The *Argo* swung to the east, with the angry Sirens swimming in close pursuit.

CHAPTER 29

ZEUS AND DEMETER STRUGGLED TO KEEP their heads above the waterline in the helmet. It was now nearly completely flooded. Their only breathing space was a cramped air pocket, which kept shifting position as Proteus towed them to the gloomy depths.

"Where's Proteus taking us?" Demeter asked.

"I hope it's not back to Poseidon's throne," Zeus said glumly as he treaded water. "I don't want to drown on Poseidon's throne."

"Oh, you won't die on the throne," Proteus rasped between the powerful pulses of his eight legs. "You two will make the perfect snack for Scylla. My pet loves cracking shells and getting to the tasty meat inside."

"Uh-huh, good for it." Zeus tried to sound unconcerned while he fingered the latch on the faceplate hatch. He wasn't sure opening it at this depth would actually help matters—if he could open it at all.

Proteus came to a halt above Poseidon's throne. The dive helmet floated slowly above him, like a helium balloon at the end of its string. "Where is my beast, anyway?" Proteus wondered aloud. "Surely Scylla has dealt with Poseidon and the air-breathing war god by now."

Out of the gloom, a small harp struck Proteus on his bulbous head. "What the …?" He shook it away but saw that other wreckage was drifting by. Zeus and Demeter recognized the debris as the statuary from outside Poseidon's throne area, except now it was in pieces. "Pretty much what you'd expect from humans pretending to be us," Zeus mused.

Proteus pulsed into motion, following the trail of drifting statue accessories to Poseidon's courtyard. When the light suddenly dimmed, Proteus, Demeter, and Zeus all looked up to see Scylla's slimy body blocking out the faint sun far above. The beast was charging down the path of glittering rocks with a tan-colored lump clinging to its hide.

"It's Ares!" Demeter exclaimed.

"And he's got your sea monster right where he wants it!" Zeus taunted Proteus.

"Humph," Proteus scoffed. "Your war god is no more than a barnacle, a nuisance!" He took off in Scylla's wake, jerking the helmet roughly by its air hose. "Come, we'll go scrape him off!"

Zeus and Demeter spun and tumbled in the flooded helmet.

CHAPTER 30

POSEIDON DODGED JAGGED BOULDERS AND dove under overhangs as he sprinted alongside the rocky base of the familiar seamount, keeping just ahead of Scylla. He heard a crash and peeked behind him to find that the monster had simply smashed through those same rocks and overhangs—and was now just inches from his tail fins. Scylla lurched forward, trying to grasp Poseidon with its suckers. The handle of Poseidon's trident, which was still stuck firmly in the center of Scylla's face, poked the pufferfish and spurred him faster. Puffing hard, Poseidon called to Ares. "Perhaps you could slow the serpent down? I'll never make it to the jaws at this rate."

"Otay," Ares mumbled around a mouthful of Scylla

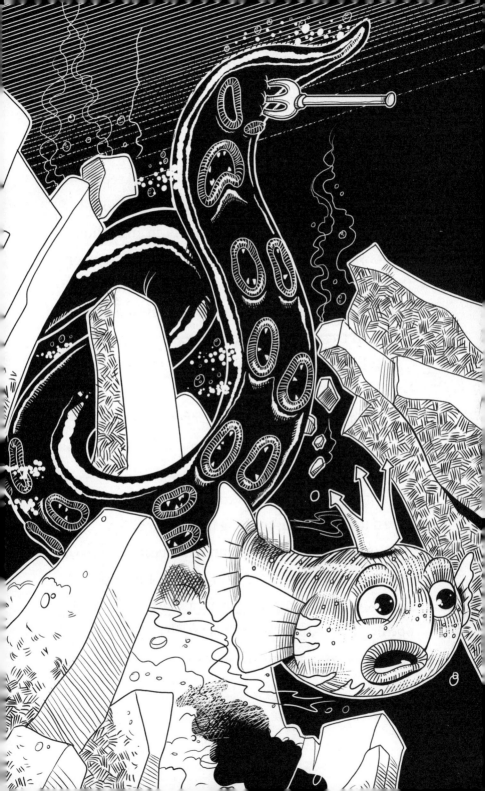

skin. He dug his back paws into the sea bottom and chomped with all his might.

Behind them, unseen, Proteus pumped his tentacles with raw fury. Yet he wasn't fast enough to keep up— let alone pluck Ares from Scylla's hide. The flooded helmet he towed might as well have been an anchor. He considered morphing into a faster sea creature, one that was all fins, but there was a problem with that idea. "That would mean letting you two go," he mused to Zeus and Demeter in his raspy voice.

"What'd he say?" Demeter strained to hear. "He's letting us go?"

Up ahead, Scylla suddenly slackened its pace and rotated its body, trying to snag Ares on the seamount's rocky surface.

With the pug so close, Proteus saw his chance and bolted toward Scylla, yanking the helmet along.

Poseidon, still in full sprint, was focused on the wall of the seamount to his right. "There!" He'd spotted a narrow gap in the rock. He made a sharp turn into the opening and found himself in a familiar dim canyon above an abyss. Hoping the monster had followed him,

Poseidon glanced backward and watched Scylla shoot past the entrance. "Drat!" he muttered.

But before he could make a move, Scylla suddenly smashed through the opening. Ares, miraculously, still clung to the beast as it raced toward Poseidon. Relieved that Scylla was still in pursuit, Poseidon charged deeper into the canyon.

Proteus had nearly overshot Scylla when the beast made its sudden turn. He put on the brakes, sending Zeus and Demeter swirling through the helmet water. Proteus just caught sight of the monster's endless body slithering into a gap in the seamount's side. "The poor beast is trying to scrape off Ares," he mused. "Coming, my pet!" He pulsed back up to speed and dove for Scylla's underbelly, dragging Zeus and Demeter through the rocky opening.

Zeus saw that they were once again over the glowing lava abyss. He nudged Demeter. "I think I know where we're going," he whispered. "And if we're going where I think we're going, I think we'll be very happy we're going there."

"Shush back there!" Proteus roared. Ares's stocky

rump was nearly within his reach. "I'd hate for you two to waste your last breath before Scylla's snack time!" He reached two tentacles toward the pug, who was too preoccupied with hanging on to Scylla to notice the looming threat behind him.

Zeus and Demeter tried to warn Ares, but the last of their air had disappeared. The helmet had completely filled with water. Zeus shut his eyes against the stinging seawater and pressed his paws on the faceplate, feeling blindly for the latch he knew was there. He grabbed one of Demeter's legs instead. Squinting through one eye, Zeus saw that Demeter was searching for the latch, too.

Together they grabbed it and pulled, bracing themselves against the helmet wall for leverage. The latch started to give way, but then stopped. The faceplate remained shut.

CHAPTER 31

STILL IN THE LEAD, POSEIDON FINALLY spotted the white glint he'd been heading for— the secret entrance to the Santorini shortcut. He didn't need to check behind him to know Scylla was close. The handle of his trident, still stuck in Scylla's face, was tickling his tail fins. On the point of exhaustion, he dug deep for one final burst of speed. The white glint resolved quickly into the massive shark jaws. Poseidon swam through them and banked out of sight. He turned in time to watch the sucker-tipped head of Scylla shoot through the jaws, followed by its endless slimy body, which was svelte enough to avoid being raked by the arrowhead teeth.

Poseidon was prepared to spring his trap. He waited

as Scylla's rubbery body continued through the jaws. Soon, Ares came into view. The war god was still clinging to the hide of Scylla, but something else had attached itself to the war god. Poseidon didn't have time to ponder. He reached a fin down and triggered the jaws' locking mechanism, snapping them shut.

The water realm exploded in bubbles.

The jaws had cut cleanly through Scylla, severing its sucker-covered body. This front part of the creature shot toward the surface in wild loops and corkscrews, rocketed by a stream of air, like a balloon deflating. Ares remained clamped to the beast's hide, enjoying one last wild ride. And hugging the pug's meatloaf-shaped body was ... "Proteus?" Poseidon couldn't believe it. The shape-changing octopus clung defiantly to Ares with all eight of his tentacles.

THOMP. Something heavy landed on the sandy seafloor behind Poseidon. He spun. It was his dive helmet, battered, cracked, and filled with cloudy seawater. There was no sign of Zeus or Demeter. He swam closer to inspect it. The faceplate was missing.

CHAPTER 32

THE ARGO CRUISED SLOWLY EAST, HERMES
working the oars as they crested rolling swells.

Athena, her forehead furrowed in concentration,
scanned the surface for any sign of the other Olympians.
The frustrated Sirens still swirled around them. Hermes
batted them aside with the oars when they got too close.
After a while, they started to keep their distance, orbiting
the boat out of oar range.

Finally, Athena spotted a stream of tiny bubbles in
front of them. She padded to the deck's edge to investigate.
"SOMETHING'S GOING ON DOWN THERE!" she
shouted. She had kept the feathers in her ears in case
the Sirens restarted their tune.

"DON'T HAVE TO YELL," Hermes reminded her.

KASPLOOSH! The stream erupted into a giant spray of massive bubbles, soaking Athena's gray fur. In the midst of the bubbles emerged Ares. "Hello, fellow Olympians," he said nonchalantly as he dog-paddled easily through the roiling water.

"Buddy!" Hermes said happily. "Where ya been?"

"Socializing with Scylla." Ares kicked onto his back amid shreds of dark, rubbery hide—the remnants of Scylla—bobbing around him.

"Seems like y'all socialized pretty hard," Hermes said, as one particularly large shred drifted by.

Embedded in it was a familiar artifact. "What's this doing here?" Hermes reached overboard and plucked it free.

"POSEIDON'S TRIDENT?" Athena exclaimed when she saw the artifact. "WHAT'S THAT DOING HERE?"

"Why are you yelling, Athena?" Ares asked as he swam to the side of the *Argo* and prepared to climb aboard. Both Hermes and Athena tensed, ready to balance the boat so Ares wouldn't swamp it. But the pug pulled himself onto the deck with surprising grace. The *Argo* didn't even wobble.

Hermes relaxed her stance and whistled in amazement. "You got your sea legs right quick, pal."

Athena's eyes narrowed as she watched Ares pad to the middle of the deck without even shaking off.

Noticing that Ares was aboard, the Sirens tightened their frenzied circle and resumed their hypnotizing tune.

At the same time, a second Ares broke the surface next to the *Argo*, panting hard. "Oh, hey everybody," he sputtered as he dog-paddled clumsily.

"Buddy?" Hermes replied, confused.

"NOT AGAIN!" shouted Athena.

The Sirens had reached full volume. Hermes saw that both Areses—the one in the water and the one on the *Argo*—were becoming dazed. "ARES!" she screamed at both in a voice even louder than Athena's, "THE FEATHERS! REMEMBER THE FEATHERS!"

"Feathers?" both dazed Areses repeated. The Ares on deck simply stared at Hermes, but the Ares in the water shook the fog from his head, trying to think. "Right! The feathers!" He pulled a soggy clump of Hermes's speckled feathers from beneath his spiked collar and quickly crammed them into his floppy ears. "THAT'S BETTER!" He floated on his back in the swell and giggled. "THESE THINGS TICKLE! HOW DO YOU WEAR THEM ALL OVER YOUR BODY?"

"YOU DON'T HAVE TO YELL. I CAN HEAR YOU JUST—" Hermes was cut off by a wet splat next to her. She turned to find a striped octopus sound asleep in a heap on the deck of the *Argo*. The first Ares was nowhere in sight. One of the octopus tentacles fell across Hermes's feet. "Uck!" she leapt back. Then noticed how quiet it was.

The Sirens had abruptly cut off their song, aghast that they had hypnotized their master. "Wake up, wake up, wake up, my lord!" they chanted in unison.

The octopus began stirring.

"Oh no you don't!" Hermes slipped her silver chain over her head, undid its latch, and quickly wrapped it around the octopus's legs, cinching them tight. The creature struggled against its bonds, despite still being dazed by his own minions' song.

"FASCINATING." Athena was sniffing at the writhing octopus, examining his true form. "SO THIS IS—"

"Proteus?" shouted Zeus from far away. "You captured Proteus!"

Hermes, Athena, and Ares all turned to find Zeus and Demeter approaching fast from a distance.

Somehow they appeared to be walking on the surface of the water.

CHAPTER 33

I **GUESS ZEUS IS THE TYPE OF GOD THAT**
can walk on water after all," Hermes mused.

As Zeus and Demeter neared, the other
Olympians realized they weren't actually treading on
the sea's surface. They were standing on a floating piece
of clear, curved material. Athena recognized it first.
"IT'S THE FACEPLATE TO POSEIDON'S HELMET."

"Why are you yelling, Athena?" asked Demeter. She
held tightly to a rope attached to something ahead of
them in the water—something kicking up a small wake.

"Where's Poseidon?" Ares had dog-paddled out to
meet them.

"Here!" the pufferfish said, rising to the surface.
He noticed the Sirens chanting for their master and

quickly called to his own minions. "Arion! Shoo away Proteus's Sirens!"

The seahorses had been towing the faceplate using the line that Demeter held. Upon hearing Poseidon's command, Arion and his team exploded into action, releasing Zeus and Demeter's raft and letting it drift to a stop. It didn't take long for the Sirens to dash into the deep. They left two distinct incandescent wakes as the seahorses chased them away.

"GUESS WE WON'T NEED THESE ANYMORE." Athena plucked the feathers from her ears.

"Thank the gods," Hermes muttered.

Poseidon took up the tow rope and pulled the faceplate alongside the *Argo*. Zeus and Demeter hopped aboard, followed by Ares, who joined them much less gracefully than his doppelgänger had. Like Athena, he pulled the feathers from his ears.

Poseidon watched the faceplate drift away on the current. "I'm going to need another helmet, I'm afraid." He held up his empty fins. "And a new trident."

"Nah, this one still works." Hermes tossed the trident she'd fished from the water to a surprised Poseidon.

He brandished it proudly and puffed up with emotion.

Zeus shuffled to the center of the crowded deck. His sopping fur was matted with grime, although his chiton was as immaculate and dry as ever. "I've had enough Oddest Sea adventures to last a decade, but I guess we still have some unfinished business here." He stood over the bound, writhing form of Proteus.

The octopus was now fully alert. "Oh, there are far more dangerous adventures ahead for you, Zeus," Proteus rasped. "Remember that war I mentioned?"

Zeus shrugged. He reached down and began hauling the octopus toward the edge of the deck.

"War?" Athena sounded alarmed. "Demeter, what's Proteus talking about?"

"Proteus peeked into our future when he had us tied up down there," Demeter explained. "He said he'd never seen anything so bleak."

"War with who?" Poseidon asked.

"Who cares?" Zeus was still pulling Proteus by Hermes's chain. "Let's dump this loudmouth. I'm tired and want to go home."

"No, no, no," Poseidon insisted. "You're not dumping that rascal back into my realm."

"War with who?" Athena repeated. She stepped in front of Zeus, blocking him from tossing the octopus overboard. "We lulled you to sleep and caught you fair and square, Proteus," she said. "According to your rules, you have to tell us our future."

"This is such a waste of time." Zeus threw up his arms and stomped to the middle of the deck, where he sat down in a huff.

The striped octopus's beady eyes darted to the

sea's surface around the *Argo*.

"If yer lookin' for yer sleepy-time gang," Hermes said, crossing her wings, "they skedaddled."

Proteus ceased struggling and shrank, resigned to his fate. "Very well," he muttered. "You captured me, so I am obligated to reveal your future. Although you will wish I hadn't."

All the Olympians except Zeus had gathered around him on the crowded deck. Hermes leaned over and removed the chain binding Proteus's tentacles.

"Tell us our future!" Ares said excitedly. "Tell us! Tell us!"

"I don't *tell* anything," Proteus explained, his skin suddenly shifting colors. "I *show* it." He closed his eyes as his body began to change textures and shapes.

CHAPTER 34

THENA, ARES, HERMES, AND DEMETER
backed up to give Proteus room.

"What's he up to?" Poseidon asked from the water.

"If this goes like last time," Demeter explained, "he's going to morph into a bunch of objects, and I think they're supposed to reveal our future somehow."

"You mean it's up to us to figure out what the objects represent?" Athena asked.

"Ooh, like a game of charades!" Ares spun in a circle. "I love charades."

"Last time he turned into a horsey," Zeus offered. "So have fun figuring that one out." He was relaxing on the deck, with his paws folded behind his head, ignoring

Proteus's shape-shifting display.

The octopus had begun to jerk and pulsate with gusto. It soon took on a new form. That of a door bearing a strange script.

Coming Soon:
Mount Olympus
Pet Center
Expansion

"Ooh, ooh, a door!" Ares barked excitedly.

"Our future is ... a door?" Athena tilted her head.

"I'd swear that's the door to uncharted territory," Demeter said.

"This is one weird game of charades." Hermes rubbed her rubbery chin waddle.

Proteus's door suddenly seemed to burst open, then melted into an inky black glob. The glob became a round shape—a vessel, similar to the *Argo* but stouter. Its deck crawled with an assortment of unfamiliar animals.

The Olympians exchanged confused glances. "Any guesses?" Demeter asked.

"I got nothin'." Ares scratched at his collar.

"Whoever those critters are," Hermes offered, "they ain't us."

Then the vessel seemed to soften around the edges. It morphed into another blob that sprouted four hoofed legs before resolving into a large land animal.

"A horsey!" Ares exclaimed. "Hey, Zeus, Proteus is showing the horsey again!"

Before Zeus could respond, the horse split down its middle and a small figure dropped out of it, brandishing a lightning bolt in one hand and a bucket-shaped helmet in the other. Even though the figure's skin was a mottled black, his identity was unmistakable.

"Zeus?" the Olympians asked in unison.

"Yeah?" Zeus propped himself up on his elbows just in time to see his mini doppelgänger slip the bucket-like helmet over his head and vanish. Proteus resumed his original form and lay panting in an inky puddle.

"Was that ... was that an itty-bitty me?" Zeus was on his feet.

"Is that the end of your future-telling show?" Athena asked Proteus.

"I hope it's followed by a question-and-answer session," Demeter added.

"I ... I honored my obligation," the octopus said weakly. "I foretold your future. Now please ... just let me go."

Out in the water, Poseidon puffed in outrage. "Let you go? So you can go find your minions and try to retake my realm?"

Proteus sagged even further into himself. "I've lost any desire to rule your kingdom, Poseidon." He rolled onto his back. "Now that I've seen the full picture of your future, all I want to do is leave this place."

The Olympians on deck looked toward Poseidon.

"We've beaten you and your cohorts, Proteus," the pufferfish said. "I could command my minions to throw you into an abyss as punishment for all the trouble you've caused. But you seem to have learned not to tangle with the Olympians." He brandished his trident. "You may go."

The Olympians aboard the *Argo* parted to make a path for Proteus. "I suppose I should have seen this coming," the octopus replied as he slipped into the water. He resurfaced with a smirk. "Enjoy your little war. I'll be waiting to pick up the pieces on my island of Pharos."

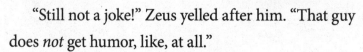

With one last deep, raspy laugh, Proteus sank below the waves.

"Still not a joke!" Zeus yelled after him. "That guy does *not* get humor, like, at all."

The other Olympians were silent.

"I won't miss him," Hermes finally said.

"War." Poseidon repeated. "I still don't get it. War with who?"

"Do you think it had something to do with those little animals Proteus showed us?" Demeter asked.

Everyone turned to Zeus, who was staring at the glinting surface of the water where Proteus had disappeared. That's when it dawned on him: The water was glistening in the sun. Daybreak! "Olympians!" he exclaimed. "We have to go home, now! Artie and Callie will be back in Greece at any minute!"

"Zeus is right," Poseidon said. "You must all leave my realm while you can. And I must clean up the messes that Proteus left me." He waved his trident in salute and disappeared beneath the surface.

Athena hopped to the tiller. "Hermes, Ares, get busy on the oars! We need to reach shore before Artie gets here!"

The *Argo*'s deck wobbled as the pug and hen hopped into action.

CHAPTER 35

"**ABANDON SHIP!" ATHENA ORDERED AS** soon as her boat skidded up to the shore. Zeus, Demeter, Hermes, Ares, and finally Athena all leapt from the *Argo*'s deck onto a stack of seaside crates, then down to solid ground. They heard a *GLUG* and turned to see the *Argo* list, then founder.

"Ah, see, I *knew* we should've added a figurehead!" Hermes shook her head.

"She was a good ship," Athena murmured. The *Argo* quietly dipped beneath the surface and settled on the shallow bottom of the Aegean.

"Yeah, yeah, the best ship, yada, yada," Zeus said as he shook his fur dry. "Now can we figure out how to get Demeter and me back home?"

The Olympians stood in a circle. Mount Olympus seemed impossibly high from their vantage point.

"Will those help?" Demeter asked, pointing at the tubes they had used to launch the *Argo ½*.

"Hamster tunnels, right?" Hermes added. "That's what Callie called them. Seems like your own tunnel would come in handy right now."

"Worth a shot!" Zeus shouted. He tugged at a length of tubing, sending it crashing down from the sea's edge. "Heavier than they look!" he added. "Ares, a little help?"

"We'll all help," Athena offered. Soon, with great effort—and some trial and error—the Olympians had managed to connect several tube sections into one long, rickety tunnel that ran from the ground to the summit of Mount Olympus.

Zeus and Demeter hesitated at the wobbly-looking tunnel's entrance. "After you, Zeus," Demeter offered.

Ignoring her, he reached out a paw and gently nudged the tunnel to test its stability. The structure shimmied from top to bottom.

"Hey, that thing can't be any sketchier than Escape Plan Icarus," Hermes said.

"Or Escape Plan Neptune!"
Ares added.

"It's the best we could do,"
Athena said. "You've got to get
back up to your palace. Now."

"Okay, okay! Here goes." Zeus
entered the tunnel and scurried up
and up, Demeter following close. It
rocked worryingly from side to side,
but before they knew it, they emerged
on Mount Olympus. Zeus took a
moment to savor his return home.

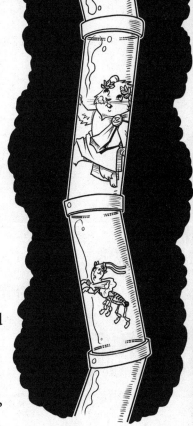

Demeter tapped Zeus's arm. "Um,
we should get back to the palace."

The duo muscled the tunnel off the summit, letting
it smash back into pieces on the floor. They dashed
through the broken back door of Zeus's palace and
carefully arranged it on its hinges. Demeter curled up
in a corner as Zeus dove onto his Golden Fleece bed
and feigned sleep.

Just in time: Artie and Callie had walked through
the door of Mount Olympus Pet Center.

CHAPTER 36

ZEUS EXPECTED THE WORST: ARTIE and Callie would know the shattered tubing had helped him and Demeter climb home. They would find the sunken *Argo*. Or wonder why Proteus, whom they obviously cared about, was nowhere to be seen.

Instead, neither of them went about their normal morning routine. Callie remained at the front entrance. Artie, meanwhile, held her black device in front of her face, speaking to it as if she were addressing a crowd.

"What's Artie saying?" Demeter peeked over the Golden Fleece.

"Shush!" Zeus hissed, trying to listen.

"Today is the big day!" Artie was announcing.

"Today, Mount Olympus Pet Center is doubling in size!" She gave Callie a thumbs-up. Callie returned it.

"Haven't we had enough changes?" Demeter groused.

"Today," Artie continued, "our expansion is officially ready for business!" She opened the portal to uncharted territory. The calls of strange animals—dogs, cats, birds—filtered through it.

Zeus's stomach dropped.

"Welcome to Mount Olympus Two-Point-Oh," Artie said happily. "Henceforth, our expansion shall be known as ... Sparta!"

Callie nodded. "I like it."

"I don't like it." Zeus tried to see into the portal, but Artie blocked his view.

"Sparta? What's that, Zeus?" Demeter nibbled nervously on a fresh lettuce sash. "Is this related to what Proteus showed us, the door and the war and all that?"

Zeus scanned Greece, taking in all its splendor, its rugged mountains and glittering, newly expanded sea. Artie had mentioned doubling her center in size. But his realm suddenly felt smaller. "Demeter, I'm afraid we're going to find out."

THE TRUTH BEHIND THE FICTION

Myths on the Map

Ancient Greece was both a time and a place—a civilization that flourished near the Aegean and Mediterranean Seas around 2,500 years ago. It was a realm of heroic mortals ruled by fearsome gods who didn't always get along. Or so Greek mythology would have us believe. How seriously should we take these myths? Are they history lessons or fairy tales? Actually, they're a bit of both.

What Is a Myth?

A myth is a special kind of story that tries to explain something. Myths helped people make sense of their world in the days before science and internet search engines. Why does the sun set? Why does the earth shake? Where did the world come from? Myths offered supernatural solutions to these mysteries by explaining that a gaggle of gods and goddesses controlled them. Ancient Greeks took these stories for fact, building temples and holding lavish events to appease

Olympian gods had their own colossal temples. This one was built for Zeus in Athens, Greece, and once had more than a hundred columns.

the gods. The original Olympic games were created in honor of Zeus, king of the gods.

The Mythmakers

No one knows who first came up with the Greek myths. The tales weren't written down until around 800 B.C., when a poet named Homer composed his two epic poems, *The Iliad* and *The Odyssey* (which inspired the plot of this book). The stories were an account of a conflict called the Trojan War and featured Greek gods and mortal humans. The ancient Greeks already knew all about these characters from their own songs and poems.

To Be Continued ...

Even after the civilization of ancient Greece fell under Roman rule more than 2,000 years ago, Greek culture lived on and its myths were not forgotten. The Romans simply adapted them for their own use. Modern day authors, playwrights, and screenwriters do the same thing, tweaking and retelling myths for audiences.

Today, Greek mythology's influence can be found everywhere, from movies to store names to clothing brands. The Greeks' myths established the "hero's journey"—a formula featured in stories ranging from *Star Wars* to *Harry Potter*: a hero yearning for adventure, a series of dangerous trials, help or hindrance from the supernatural, and victory over impossible odds. Sound familiar?

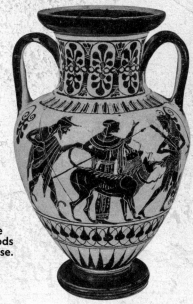

Athena marches in the middle of a parade of gods on this ancient Greek vase.

The ancient Greeks worshipped 12 major gods known as the Olympians (because they gathered on Mount Olympus, the highest peak in ancient Greece). These gods were all-powerful, and yet they possessed the same emotions—love, sadness, anger, jealousy—as everyday mortals.

Zeus

King of the gods, Zeus ruled from Mount Olympus and held domain over the heavens and the land beneath them. He brought order, making sure none of the Olympians got out of line.

Poseidon

God of all bodies of water, Poseidon commanded the tides using his enchanted trident. Sailors prayed to him for safe passage. He was a brother of Zeus. Like some siblings, they didn't always get along.

Hades

Another brother of Zeus, Hades chose the mysterious realm of the Underworld for his kingdom. There he sat on his bronze throne and ruled over an odd assortment of monsters and mortals. They were welcome to enter his land of the dead, but they could never leave.

Athena

Goddess of wisdom, Athena was the brains of the Olympian operation. She also inspired creativity. When ancient Greeks wanted to build something, they prayed to Athena for inspiration.

Ares

Few Greek gods were as feared as Ares, the god of war. He was a brute, a force of chaos. He attacked first and asked questions ... never! Warriors screamed his name before charging into battle.

Demeter

As the goddess of food and the harvest, Demeter was beloved by ancient Greeks. One bad season of crops could lead to disaster. Demeter kept everyone's belly full.

Artemis

A guardian and caretaker, Artemis was the goddess of animals, protecting the young and helpless. She lived in the wilderness, tending to her furry and feathered friends.

Hermes

With his feathered sandals and winged hat, Hermes was the most graceful of the Olympian gods, which is one reason they chose him as their messenger. Mortals prayed to him when they needed wit, trickery, or even a good night's sleep.

MEET THE VILLAINS

Beware these troublemakers who inhabit our tale ...

Proteus

Although this shepherd of the sea was a minion of Poseidon, he had godlike powers: Proteus could read the future and morph from an old man into any creature he chose. But Proteus only offered his predictions if he was caught and bound during his midday nap.

The Sirens

These half-bird, half-human sea nymphs combined their beautiful voices together into a hypnotic chorus that lured drowsy sailors to their doom against the rocks.

The Myth of the Odyssey

Hercules is the man with the muscles. Achilles is history's greatest warrior. But the most admired Greek hero of all could be a guy you've barely heard of: Odysseus. He was the ruler of the island kingdom of Ithaca, but he was really just an ordinary Joe—not particularly strong, not an unstoppable super soldier. But Odysseus was crafty, and his cunning helped him survive the most frustrating voyage in history.

A Hero's Journey

Odysseus's tale is recounted in *The Iliad* and *The Odyssey*, epic poems about a 10-year war in the region that Odysseus fought in. But the real adventure unfolded during his journey home from the war. It should have been a short, easy voyage to Ithaca and his family. But the gods were against Odysseus. The seas were plagued with monsters, storms, and other perils. His trip ended up taking 10 years.

The Oddest Seas

Odysseus's voyage got off to a terrible start when a storm blew his small fleet of ships off course and out to sea. Starving, Odysseus and his crew stopped at an island and found a cave full of chubby sheep—fresh meat! But the flock was guarded by a one-eyed giant known as the Cyclops. The brawny monster came out swinging a massive wooden club. Quick-thinking Odysseus ordered his men to cling to the sheeps' bellies so they couldn't be seen. They escaped safely when the sheep walked out of the cave.

Once back at sea, Odysseus and his crew heard a haunting chorus of lovely voices drifting on the wind. It was a hypnotizing tune, and soon they began drooping into a state of forgetfulness. Odysseus recognized the chorus's source—the Sirens, naughty sea nymphs that were famous for lulling sailors to their doom. Odysseus cleverly stuffed his ears with beeswax and instructed the others to do the same.

The journey continued, and soon they had to pass through a narrow stretch of sea guarded by monsters. Odysseus had to choose between an encounter with Charybdis, a living whirlpool, or Scylla, a serpent with a bottomless appetite. He took his chances with Scylla, hoping his zippy fleet could outrun the tentacled creature. Odysseus and his vessel survived, but six of his sailors did not.

Unstoppable Odysseus

The misadventures continued. On one remote island, a witch transformed his crew into pigs. Odysseus resisted the spell thanks to an antidote supplied by the god Hermes. Odysseus forced the witch to restore his piggy friends to people. The storms and magical attacks continued until only Odysseus remained, adrift, alive because of his wits. And that is why he was so beloved by the ancient Greeks. They idolized his cunning. He was an average mortal in a world of gods and monsters, but despite the constant dangers and frustrations, Odysseus never gave up, never let his guard down, never stopped thinking his way out of every problem.

Finally, 20 years after he'd left for the Trojan War, Odysseus made it back to Ithaca. His family cried tears of joy. They had never given up hope that he would return. Even his dog remembered him. Odysseus was home.

Inset map caption:

Athens, Greece

Athens, Georgia, United States

Athens, Georgia, is about 5,600 miles (9,000 km) away from Athens, Greece.

SERBIA

KOSOVO

NORTH MACEDONIA

ALBANIA

Mount Olympus

GREECE

ITALY

ADRIATIC SEA

IONIAN SEA

TYRRHENIAN SEA

Delphi

Corinth

Nemea

Argos

Sparta

Taenarum

Strait of Messina

SICILY

According to mythology, Scylla the sea monster lurked in a seaside cave on the Strait of Messina off the coast of modern-day Italy. The other side of the strait was inhabited by Charybdis the whirlpool monster. Sailors navigating this passage had to run the gauntlet of both fearsome monsters.

Ancient Greece was a sprawling civilization of independent city-states. While its geography divided it into many separate regions, they all shared the same language, culture, and—most important—mythology.

MAP KEY

◆ Ancient location

● Ancient city

▮ Area considered ancient Greece around 750 B.C.

— Present-day boundary

To Colchis →

BULGARIA

BLACK SEA

The highest peak in ancient Greece, Mount Olympus was home to Zeus and was where he held court over the Olympians.

Sea of Marmara

TÜRKİYE (TURKEY)

A tourist hot spot today, the Tunnel of Eupalinos is more than 3,000 feet (1 km) long and was dug through a mountain on the island of Samos around the sixth century B.C. as an aqueduct, or system for transporting water. It's one of the oldest human-made tunnels in history and appears in several Greek myths.

Troy •

AEGEAN SEA

• Thebes

• Athens

Tunnel of Eupalinos ◆

Miletus •

The island of Santorini was born of fire and molten rock, starting as an underwater mountain—called a seamount—that formed from a volcanic eruption. According to Greek mythology, Santorini, also known as Thera, was created by one of Poseidon's sons, who tossed a ball of earth into the sea.

Santorini ◆

Sea of Crete

CRETE

• **Knossos**

| 0 | | 100 miles |
| 0 | | 100 kilometers |

MEDITERRANEAN SEA

189

GREEKING OUT

"Welcome back to Greeking Out, your podcast that delivers the goods on Greek gods and epic tales of triumphant heroes. I'm your host, the Oracle of Wi-Fi. We have a special announcement for all mythology megafans.

If you love the tales in Zeus the Mighty, you'll be blown away by the spectacular stories in the upcoming National Geographic Kids book Greeking Out: Epic Retellings of Classic Greek Myths, inspired by the hit Greeking Out podcast.

Let me introduce ... the titans of tales! The world's most magnificent monsters! And the legendary heroes that, well, invented the term "legends." Want a sneak peek of one of the myths? Great. Just hold on to your laurel crowns ..."

The True Story of That Famous Flying Horse

Bellerophon wanted to fly Pegasus all the way up to the top of Mount Olympus. As he fixed the saddle to Pegasus, Bellerophon could see the concern in his friend's eyes. "Not to worry, old boy," he reassured the horse. "I will be welcome at Olympus."

Pegasus knew this wouldn't end well. He bucked and reared as Bellerophon climbed on his back. But the rider held fast and soon the pair were soaring above the clouds, headed right for the gates of Mount Olympus.

Naturally, Zeus had heard all of this and was not happy about it at all.

"He thinks he belongs here among the Gods!" Zeus exclaimed angrily. "A few fights on a flying horse, and all of a sudden he's as good as Zeus?!"

He reached for his thunderbolts, preparing to knock the hero off his horse and out of the sky. Poseidon tried to convince Zeus that Bellerophon meant no offense—he was just curious. Athena pointed out that Pegasus would look really good pulling Zeus's chariot.

"Fine," said the king of the gods, "I will not strike him down with my thunderbolts."

The other gods breathed a sigh of relief and relaxed for a moment, until Zeus said, "But who can tell what a gadfly will do?"

And then he opened his hand and released a tiny fly into the sky ...

Greeking Out: Epic Retellings of Classic Greek Myths hits shelves in September 2023!

Acknowledgments

Like any Greek myth, the creation of Zeus the Mighty was its own odyssey, complete with a cast of indispensable fellow travelers. Becky Baines at National Geographic Kids dreamed up the idea of Mount Olympus Pet Center and invited me to embark on this quest. Catherine Frank—oracle of children's literature—always finds the most exciting narrative paths for us to explore. Nat Geo's Avery Naughton keeps us from losing our way.

Illustrator Andy Elkerton continues to bring our Olympian heroes (and their nefarious foes) to vivid life, while design director Amanda Larsen creates the cool look for each book. Production editor Molly Reid makes sure the world of Mount Olympus Pet Center is portrayed consistently from the first page to the last. Photo director Lori Epstein lends her expert eye.

Dr. Diane Harris Cline, a professor of history and classics at George Washington University, is my beacon for staying within range of the source material. She's written the book on ancient Greece. Literally. It's called *The Greeks: An Illustrated History,* and it was as valuable to me in this adventure as any of Zeus's relics.

I inherited my love of reading from my mom, Sue, at an early age. Finally, my wife, Ramah, is an endless source of inspiration and patience. She's also the wisest person I know when it comes to animals (we live on a farm). We currently have more than 20 chickens (including a hen named Hermes), four geese, four sheep, two cows, and a donkey. I'm starting to suspect that, like Zeus and the Olympians, these animals believe they're mythological gods and go on nightly adventures.

—*Crispin Boyer*

All artwork by Andy Elkerton/Shannon Associates; 182, Pamela Loreto Perez/Shutterstock; 183 (UP), kanvag/Shutterstock; 183 (LO), Rogers Fund, 1906/Metropolitan Museum of Art; 184 (UP LE), DeAgostini/Getty Images; 184 (UP CTR), Luisa Ricciarini/Leemage/Universal Images Group/Getty Images; 184 (UP RT), Gift of George Blumenthal, 1941/Metropolitan Museum of Art; 184 (LO LE), Harris Brisbane Dick Fund, 1950/Metropolitan Museum of Art; 184 (LO RT), Prisma Archivo/Alamy Stock Photo; 185 (UP LE), Adam Eastland/Alamy Stock Photo; 185 (UP CTR), The Cesnola Collection, Purchased by subscription, 1874-76/Metropolitan Museum of Art; 185 (UP RT), Fletcher Fund, 1925/Metropolitan Museum of Art; 185 (LO LE), Reading Room 2020/Alamy Stock Photo; 185 (LO RT), Ulysses and the Sirens, illustration from an antique Greek vase (colour litho) by French School, (19th century); Bibliotheque des Arts Decoratifs, Paris, France; © Archives Charmet/Bridgeman Images; 186, DEA/G. Dagli Orti/De Agostini via Getty Images; 186-187 (BACKGROUND), Andrey Kuzmin/Shutterstock